DARK HANDS

A Dark Medical Fantasy Romance

CK Franco

Blurbs

DARK HANDS

A Dark Medical Fantasy Romance

Dr. Alex Reid was never meant to wield darkness.

By day he's a brilliant doctor.
By night, a strange power pulses through his hands—cold, alive, and impossible to explain.

When a dying patient rises under his touch, the hospital whispers "miracle." His rival calls him dangerous. And the nurse who sees through his walls becomes the only person he can trust as his secret grows harder to hide.

But Alex's power is changing... and so is the world around him.
If he can't control the darkness inside him, it will consume everything he's fighting to protect.

A gripping fusion of medical drama, forbidden power, and slow-burn romance.

To every healer who keeps going even when their hands shake—
and to every person who has ever fought battles no one else could see.

This story is for your shadows... and your light.

"Some powers heal.

Some powers destroy.

And some powers choose their host long before the host chooses them."

Prologue

The hospital never slept.

Even at midnight, St. Vincent's hummed with restless life—monitors chirping, vents sighing, footsteps echoing like heartbeats down its endless halls. Dr. Alex Reid walked alone through the dim-lit corridor, exhaustion dragging at his bones like chains.

The day had been brutal.

The night would be worse.

He reached the pediatric ICU and stopped.

Behind the glass, a child breathed unevenly, chest rising like a fragile wave struggling to reach shore. His numbers were falling—faster than medicine could save him.

Alex placed a trembling hand on the glass.

The darkness inside him stirred.

A shadow crawled beneath his skin—cold, electric, hungry. It pulsed through his veins like ink spreading through water. His breath hitched. His vision narrowed.

Not now.

Not here.

Not where someone could see.

But the boy gasped, his small body arching, fighting for air he could no longer reach.

And Alex moved before fear could stop him.

He entered the room, reached for the child's hand, and whispered a promise he didn't know he could keep.

The shadow inside him lunged forward—and the room dropped to a dead, breathless silence.

Then the monitors began to rise.

Steady.

Stable.

Strong.

The child opened his eyes.

But when Alex looked at his own hands...

the darkness curled around his fingertips like smoke.

And in that moment, he realized:

This wasn't a miracle.

It was the beginning.

Contents

A Doctor's Burden

Dr. Alex Reid

Sunlight falls in bright strips on the white tiles through glass panels—light too sharp to touch the skin inside this building. Sliding doors open with a soft sound, and the cold air smells faintly of cleaning supplies. As I walk, the steady hum of St. Vincent's grows louder—a feeling that starts in my feet and rises with every person moving in the halls. There is no pause here. Everyone moves quickly and with purpose: nurses in green and blue uniforms darting around, doctors' coats swinging, and even the silence between their words heavy with focus. Shoulders hunched, breath quick, I step into the flow.

People pass by—too many to count; bodies weaving, heels clicking, quiet voices rising and falling. Their shoes trace hours before the clocks catch up, and the glass walls show broken reflections of me—just a pale ghost among the living. There is no time to wait or rest, no chance to find peace between shifts. Every heartbeat challenges you here, and eyes are everywhere, always watching. No matter how tired or empty I feel, I have to keep going or be crushed by the machine's demands.

The small pain in my chest grows with each quick step. My lungs taste leftover perfume and the sharp smell of sanitizer—a mix that never fades, like the need to act as if I'm steady. Nurse Kim gives me a brief nod; Dr. Owens barely looks up, lost in charts and quiet requests. The world shrinks to a tunnel of white and blue, voices sharp with tiredness or strong with command.

The clinic doors shine ahead, lit by harsh lights. My messenger bag, heavy with files and sleepless nights, feels twice as heavy as it should. My knees shake, and the wheels of a gurney scrape the wall beside me—a brief rush of rubber, the snap of tight gloves. I set down the bag and dig through patient files, notes clipped and half-remembered orders. My fingers tremble slightly—a small but clear sign that limits exist, and my body notices.

Looking at charts, the world breaks down into numbers, names, and doses—Sam G., low white blood count; Mrs. Hendricks, fever still high; dozens of hearts beating, all waiting, trusting. A blue highlighter marks a note about Sam's next test—yellowed pages flutter in the weak breeze from a vent. I force myself to focus, jaw tight, counting the beats between breaths. Every detail matters: medicine schedules, allergies, scribbled notes. My mind narrows, blocking out the fear of missing something important.

It's not just the illness that wears me down, but this constant pressure to be perfect and sure. If I slip, a patient suffers. If I falter, someone sharper will point out how far I've fallen. Everyone here hopes, but we feed a system that uses whole people and leaves only tired halves behind. This hospital breeds competition even as it claims to heal. The line between a safe place and a battleground is blurred by the noises of machines and the ticking clocks.

Footsteps come fast and even. Dr. Marcus Flynn crosses the hall, his coat crisp and shoes shining. Doors open wider for him, people step aside. For a moment, his sharp blue eyes meet mine—no smile, just a look that cuts to the bone; doubt is clear in the small raise of his brow. He moves on, his steps smooth and quick, ignoring me like a finished stitch.

The hall fills again with the echo of his shoes. His absence darkens my thoughts. Does he see what I hide—the shadows near my bones, the struggle to stand and breathe and keep going? Or does he just see weakness, easy for everyone to spot, like blood bleeding through bandages?

I lean back against the wall, my head bowed, fatigue gathering in my chest. The hospital's pulse beats through me, my cheek cool against the hard stone. Closing my eyes, I focus on the slight shake in my hand, the uneven breath. Other mornings blur together; every new day opens a wound—the fear that one step slower, one slip, could show the hidden darkness under my skin. Healing happens in bright rooms, in kind voices and quiet moments between alarms. Behind closed eyes, though, what grows is the darkness—waiting, watching, ready.

I stand up straight, fingers fidgeting with my coat as I try to bring calm to my tired body. Life outside keeps moving—a nurse laughs, a pager rings, and life hangs by a thread in every room. I steady myself, planting my feet, refusing to fall apart. Fear shows too easily here, smelling like panic. But there is no space for that. The hospital watches, and every one of us faces judgment every morning—from the day and from each other.

My fist grips the cool metal of the ward door. I take a deep breath, one that almost hurts. Pushing the door open, I step into the busy morning—carts rattling, voices rising, the first wave of chaos. Ready or not, the day starts this way.

Emma Clarke

The hospital breathes out smells of disinfectant and coffee as daylight fills the ward. Our footsteps sound soft on the linoleum. Above us, a monitor beeps a steady rhythm, like a heartbeat but fragile. At the foot of bed 217, a young man curls under clean sheets, eyes wide—his hope thin. I rest my hand on his trembling shoulder, feeling the warmth of morning nerves and his low fever. His lips part, silent questions hanging between us, and for a moment, my own worry eases. Comfort flows through me, softly—let it reach his heart.

Alex stands beside me. His coat is messy, tired shadows beneath his eyes. He bends to check the IV line, careful, his lips pressed tight, hiding his nerves. His fingers flutter, then pause over the drip's dial. I notice a faint shake in his grip. The morning hum around us keeps the urgency low but never stops it. When our eyes meet, a small smile passes—a lifeline, a promise to hold onto each other in this endless struggle.

Behind us, the world moves on. Naomi steps into the room, shoulders straight, eyes scanning monitors before she speaks. She goes straight to the bedside, sandalwood and fresh linen scent behind her. A monitor beeps loudly—a warning—but Naomi's hands move with skill, silencing it with a quick fix. She checks the IV, then looks at me and Alex, a flicker of worry softening her focus. She hands the right tray to Alex, her fingers lingering on his wrist as if feeling for steadiness. The lines on her face deepen, but the unspoken question stays: Are you strong enough?

Her calm, capable presence warms me. This is how trust grows—not with words, but with moments where care is shown and accepted.

Naomi steps away, her footsteps fading, leaving the air thinner. Alex's weight pulls his shoulders down. My fingers fuss with the blanket—enough to hide restlessness—before I face him fully.

"Do you ever feel like the hospital's swallowing you up?" His voice is quiet, almost like a question to the bed.

"All the time," I say softly. "Some days, it feels like kindness slips through my hands no matter how hard I hold on. But that's why it matters every time we stay. We support each other. That's teamwork, right?"

He breathes out, shaky. "Sometimes it feels like it's not enough."

I watch the worry in his eyes, half-hidden fear. "But it is. If not today, then tomorrow. We make it enough together."

He nods, and the tension in his face eases just a little.

Naomi looks at me from the door—a pause, just long enough for understanding. Her look toward Alex, my small smile back, say: He's not as alone as he thinks. For now, that quiet connection holds us together—a silent promise across uncertain ground.

Outside this room, the world fights for attention: calls over the intercom, a monitor crying for help, voices sharp with urgent orders. In this hospital, full of rivalry and endless demand, our space feels different. The quiet teamwork growing here is clear if you pay attention. Where others see chaos, I see the soft support that keeps us steady—Naomi's sharp eyes, Alex's quiet strength, my gentle hands. In small moments, we offer what we can, and from that grows something stronger.

Moving through the beds, duty pulls me forward, but inside the tiredness presses in. Shifts blur, pain and loss piling up—grief from long ago still raw. Some mornings, the reflection in the mirror barely looks like the girl I once was, sunny and carefree. The pain of losing someone never truly leaves, so I carry it, drawing strength from every act of kindness. Teamwork is a stand against the competition, the doubt, even despair.

Sometimes I worry the weight will break me, afraid to show Alex or Naomi my cracks. But when Alex looks back with quiet thanks, the trembling in my hands steadies me. I am held just as I hold others.

Naomi and I move on, Alex just steps behind. Our shoulders nearly touch as sunlight filters in—three tired people, but for a moment, stronger than we seem—connected by something that can't be seen. Gratitude hums quietly in my chest, stronger than rest.

Ahead waits another bed, another chance to heal. The day moves on.

Dr. Alex Reid

The intensive care unit doors close softly behind me, cutting off the noise and bright halls. The air here is sharper, smelling of cleaning chemicals and plastic tubing, sticky with dried sweat. I put on my gloves carefully, the tight grip reminding me how easily my hands get tired. Morning light shines through strong glass, making every surface and skin almost blue-white, leaving no shadow to hide.

A young woman lies waiting, her lungs weak under her collarbones. IV drips, blinking monitors, cords everywhere; the beeping marks time passing. My tools sit on the tray—a scalpel, a central line kit (used for inserting a tube into a large vein for medicine or fluids), tape curling at the edges. My pulse races, fast and light, flapping nerves against ribs.

I tighten my jaw, holding the needle, trying to remember my best self—the self before the illness, before every move became a struggle. The needle's tip hovers. Sweat builds under my collar. My grip slips; a slight shake runs from wrist to palm—small, but on skin so thin it feels huge. I breathe fast, lungs tightening like a fist squeezing clay, and the small scar on my left hand pulses, pale under latex gloves. The needle wobbles just before the puncture.

Naomi steps in before I lose control. She moves sure and quick, her hands steady in my shaking grip. She speaks softly, not judging, "Let me." I give in, swallowing a bitter feeling. She works fast, sliding the catheter (a thin tube) into the vein easily. No words pass between us during that moment. The monitors beep as the patient's chest rises and falls steady.

I step back, the room suddenly too bright, my vision sharp at the edges. Naomi doesn't meet my eyes, letting silence cover what just happened like a soft blanket. I watch her hands, calm and confident, and feel a bitter ache, knowing that used to be me. What is a doctor if healing becomes heavy as a stone, each task a mountain? My mouth tastes faintly metallic—panic and envy mixed. Naomi tapes the line in place, writes notes, then leaves, squeezing my shoulder lightly—a touch that says: You are seen, not judged.

Through the glass, Marcus stands, arms crossed, eyes cold and sharp. On a better day, he might nod and move on. Not today. His blue stare cuts through the glass, seeing every weakness. Under his look, every flaw feels huge. Weakness on display—a show I'd pay to avoid. The air feels tight. I want to shrink, disappear under the floor.

Marcus turns away only when Naomi closes the chart. He leaves no mark but his presence—like a handprint left after a hand is gone.

I need air. The hallway is empty now, its harsh lights too honest. My shoulder hits the cold wall with a hollow sound. My fingers—clumsy and traitorous—run through my damp hair, gloves sticky now. I breathe hard, then steadier. Chest tight, lungs hungry for air.

St Vincent's is full of sharp edges—white walls, glass corners, piercing eyes. People here walk fast, like fear or guilt chase them. Here, I am both threat and target, barely outrunning the invisible monster gripping my bones. Medicine needs exactness, and I'm losing it like water slipping through hands. Maybe ambition was always a kind of fever, and I didn't know the sweat meant more than hard work. Maybe the price was too high from the start.

Inside me, frustration twists. Years of effort mean nothing if one mistake ruins everything—one shaky line, one look from Marcus, and the world shrinks to my failing body. Self-blame burns in my gut: why not stronger, steadier, why not normal? The voice that haunted me as a child—why are you so tired?—returns with Marcus's sharp face and Naomi's gentle touch. Fear lives in the empty places. There is a future where my hands grow weaker still, where patients, tough eyes, and lists of notes move on without me, my name remembered only with a silent sigh: That was the one who lost strength.

Yet beneath my ribs, a shadow stirs. The dark curls quietly, a second heartbeat, familiar but never trusted fully. What if the strange powers inside me are both curse and gift? Could they steady my hands, hide the shaking, heal what medicine cannot? Or would they simply consume me, swallowing kindness and care for skill? Some days the promise of power feels sweet like rain on dry land. Other days, it scares me more than the illness did.

Living here is a balance—walking a tightrope between who I am and who the world wants me to be. Maybe the only choice is not to fall. The urge to hide, to cover wounds and never be weak in public again, pulls at me, but it fades as my breath slows and the cold corridor keeps me steady.

The guilt is there, but so is a faint resolve. The world sees every slip—Marcus, Naomi, and the shadow beneath my skin—but today is not over. Weakness calls for reckoning, but it is not defeat. Not yet.

My shaking fingers pull off the gloves. The world rushes back—the phones ringing, distant calls for help, the soft hum of life. Time to move again.

The Hidden Darkness

Alex Carter

After midnight, St. Martin's is very quiet. The silence feels cold and heavy. I turn away from the nurse's station. The lights are dim, and the glass covers are dirty. The hallway smells like bleach and latex gloves. Tonight, the air feels sharper, colder, as if the walls are breathing with me.

My shoes scrape the tile floor. The old linoleum makes soft noises. The shadows here aren't just darkness—they gather in corners and around the lights. I walk past rooms named Exam 5, Pediatrics, Radiology. The walls seem full of the people who have been here before. Suddenly, the shadows change. They stretch and move, pulling away from the walls and ceiling, creeping toward me like fingers. The air feels thick and hard to breathe, with a strange smell like electricity and panic.

My heart beats fast. My hands inside latex gloves feel wet. It's more than nerves—there's something moving under my skin. Halfway down the hall, the supply room shines under an exit sign. My chest tightens with fear. It feels like a sharp pain inside me. I breathe fast.

I make fists, but my hands shake. In the light, a dark shadow swirls around my knuckles. It moves with my pulse, blacker than the night outside the rain-specked windows. The shadow flickers quietly. It's real, but it feels wrong. The light catches the blackness as it dances, then settles. The hallway feels too narrow now. I pull my hands behind my back and look down at the old floor.

Has anyone seen this? Am I losing my mind? Panic grows inside me at the thought that something inside me is breaking into the normal world of the hospital. This isn't just stress or nerves. There is a strange power under my skin, and it has nothing to do with medicine or logic.

I hear someone shout orders down the hall—Dr. Addison. That sound shocks me and I hurry down the corridor, away from the beat of my heart and the watching shadows. The trauma call makes my senses sharper. In OR 3, everything is bright under the strong lights: the sharp smells of blood, iodine, sweat, and fear.

I put on my mask and gloves. My hands move on their own, careful and fast, clamping, cutting, tying. I think about anatomy and hospital rules, but the black energy stays just under my skin. As I sew the last wound, my fingers tremble—not from tiredness. The cold pain pulses again, and the darkness starts to creep from my fingertips, a mist that stains the blue sheets. I get goosebumps, even while sweat drips from my forehead. Frost forms where my glove meets skin. The others don't notice; they focus on monitors and suction. But I see the shadow moving toward the end of the table.

What if this darkness takes over? What if the cold in the blood comes from me? The usual warnings about infection and losing limbs seem small compared to this. Am I sick? Cursed? Or losing my mind?

As soon as the surgery ends, I need to get away. The door clangs as I leave, my palm leaving a cold, dark print on the push bar. I stumble through bright hallways where my footsteps echo three times. I enter the quiet staff lounge with dim lights. The air smells like old coffee and leftover bagels.

I sink into a chair by the window. The old pipes hum above. I open my hands under the weak light, and shadows spill onto my palms before fading away, like breath on glass. It's amazing and scary. I wish it wasn't real. But it is—this change lives in me now, written on my skin.

The hospital feels like it's on a different level, all its urgent needs far away from the secret inside me. If someone came in, what could I say? "Look, shadows gather on my veins"? What happens to a doctor who can't trust his own body or senses?

I move my fingers as the blackness fades. Maybe I can control it with enough effort. Or maybe this is the start of the end. Either way, the secret weighs heavy in my chest.

The clock ticks loudly. Three hours left in the night. The world outside is the same—calm, practiced. But nothing feels the same inside me. The secret will stay with me until the sun comes up.

Alex Carter

My apartment smells like black coffee, cleaner, and tired dreams—like every medical student's place. The heater knocks again, breaking the quiet. It's late. The only light is from the kitchen lamp, shining on my new black leather journal. My palm is smudged with ink. The pen taps on my thumbnail. Each journal entry is neat and clinical, but the words don't quite fit: "22:19—corridor, Room 410. Flicker seen on wall. Shadow moved against the light." I write down every event with dates, times, and feelings, but the words can't capture the dark shadows curling around my wrists and chilling my bones.

We were taught that darkness lies outside—beyond rooftops, held back by lamps and hallway lights. But here, the darkness answers to me. It rises and holds on. It's spiteful in its coldness and strange, like it drinks at my fingers. The world looks bruised and odd for hours afterward. Writing in the journal feels like holding on, or maybe admitting a secret. I only had normal, rough shifts a few days ago. Now the pages count incidents like symptoms. The black shadow is not just a moment—it's ongoing. The notes and details almost bring comfort. At least my mind can be organized on paper—my hands cannot. If only someone could tell me what this means, or help me believe the words will make me normal again.

Tonight I keep watching the shadows in the kitchen corners, expecting them to move closer. The cheap light bulb flickers, making blurry edges. Nothing moves except my hand tremor. The shakiness stays, even as the adrenaline fades. I can't stop feeling like something watches me from under the appliances or beneath the fridge. No monsters under my bed anymore—only their strange shapes, always waiting for my heart to race so they can come out and play.

In the bathroom, moonlight paints cold blue stripes across the floor through the blinds. Steam rises from the faucet, tracing shapes on the old mirror. My reflection looks haunted, eyes wide and jaw tight. I turn off the bright light; only moon and memory remain. Shadows gather at my feet. I step into them, inviting the cold to come. I focus and breathe.

The shadow under my foot thickens, moving like it's alive. It creeps up my ankle, wrapping around like a black ribbon. The feeling is sharp and cold, but there's a strange thrill. My blood whispers for more. All I know is it feels normal—and part of me aches for it.

My heart pounds loudly. The more I watch, the less my foot feels mine. What am I becoming? How much can I write before the words run out, and only the feeling stays?

Midnight passes. The journal fills with shaky drawings—dark lines crossing fingers—and notes about feelings: cold burning, pressure under skin, like a bone healing. I'm tired. Every blink makes the world seem unsure.

By morning, sunlight slaps across the sheets like an accusation. My mouth is dry. My head aches, like shadows pool behind my eyes. Moving hurts. The hallway outside is silent and clean, like the hospital. I trip on the stairs, my weight doubling, knees buckling, shoulder hitting the railing. The air tastes like metal. Did I write in the journal or only draw more black loops? My hands close, tips numb. I blink slowly; my body fights every move, but I keep going.

The hospital's bright lights feel harsh. The station's clock counts time without care. The place is alive as usual, but everything feels distant. Nurse Patel's voice floats through the morning, dry and joking.

"Rough night, Alex?" Her eyes look at mine.

"My nights are always rough," I say too loud and fast, wearing a mask. My hands hide in my coat pockets, knuckles white. No one needs to know the blackness clings softly to my wrists. The need to see if any darkness spreads into my veins bites at me.

"You look pale, even for you. Are you okay?"

"I'm fine. Just another shift." I smile, holding it in place like stitches. The more I talk, the less I feel the words belong to me.

"Let me know if you need a break. Or a real coffee," she says with a smirk, already leaving.

"Yeah. I'll let you know." It's easier to fade away, letting whispers die and work fill the space.

The day drags. Everything feels colder, the edges of the world less sharp. By the end, even my voice feels fake. The first thing I do at home is sit at my desk, clutching the journal. It feels like a ritual—turning the old key, watching the dark book slip into the drawer. It belongs in darkness, waiting and holding secrets that bite. Better to keep them quiet until light or understanding comes.

Lila Hayes

The smell of hotel coffee and the buzz of many voices fill the air. Sunlight shines through the glass ceiling, making the carpet shine gold. The convention center's auditorium feels tense: focused, eager, nervous—a room full of doctors and scientists trying to understand the unknown. Hearts beat fast in the crowd. No one admits it, but everyone hopes for something impossible. Still, impossible things often fill these rooms.

On stage, lights blur faces. The air feels full of energy. Slides change: brain energy patterns, cases of children who faint, wake, and say they dreamed of floating black rivers. My voice is calm and practiced. I share findings with the careful steps of a surgeon handling difficult news. Some people watch closely; others scoff quietly. The ones who listen—that's why panels like this happen.

"In twenty percent of cases, we see short bursts of electrical activity alongside drops in temperature, but no blood flow problems," the slides say. "This suggests a non-biological cause. We need to work together to understand this." Some take notes; others frown skeptically. No one laughs outright here—the search for answers is serious.

I notice the crowd moves nervously even after the slides end. Some hold hope tightly but quietly. I know that hope—watching strange events break reality's rules, feeling both wonder and fear. For years, letters and secret emails have pointed to a pattern spanning continents. There are others like us. We meet in cold places, late-night bars at conferences, beside a sleeping child whose skin chills the air.

The air tastes sharp like electricity. This gathering has always made my pulse quicken, especially since the day glow worms appeared in a child's eye and vanished when doctors looked.

After the session, lights dim for the next talk. I pack my notes and watch for anyone who looks nervous but determined. A young man stands apart, hands deep in his pockets, shoulders tight as if ready for a hit. He watches my name badge and looks away quickly. His hospital badge reads St. Martin's. Doctors from there are usually calm and sure, but he looks worn down.

"Professor Hayes?" His voice is soft, almost lost in the noise of people leaving. "Do you have a moment? There's something you said about energy oddities..."

He trails off, his knuckles pale. Under the clean, sharp hospital smell, he carries a colder scent—like metal cooled fast, leftover from blood and ammonia. Emergency rooms leave marks on people; this one shows it clearly. He's young but looks tired in a way that goes deeper than years.

"Of course. How can I help?" We find seats near the wall. People pass, but he speaks quietly, afraid to say the word "darkness" aloud.

"I've... had episodes. My hands get cold, and shadows move where they shouldn't." His voice breaks. He presses his palms together, looks down. "It started at St. Martin's. During a shift. Blackness, moving inside me. My hands... something moves through them. It's not in any medical book I've seen."

Darkness, cold, strange movements—these words hit close. I remember cases from around the world: notes from Uppsala, voice recordings from Mumbai, and a young woman in Berlin who shed black tears as her father died. We must stay skeptical, but experience tells me there's more. I balance both every day.

"How often do you write down what happens?" I ask gently.

"I started a journal. But it's messy; sometimes I forget details. The tiredness is bad, and after, I feel like I'm outside myself for a while. I thought..." He shakes his head, full of apology.

"You did the right thing coming here." I lean in, lower my voice. "You're not alone. There are... patterns. Rare, hard to prove, but real. I've spent years gathering evidence—cases like yours from all over. Keep recording every event, no matter how small. Careful data is the best way forward."

His eyes sharpen, caught between doubt and hope. Science comforts us, a thin thread between us. I see faces from old research groups, secret emails under fake names, societies built on curiosity, not myth. More people seek answers—quietly, connected, cautious. We share our secrets like precious objects: journal pages, secondhand diagnoses, frost under fingernails, stories of children who call shadows with their cries.

He hesitates, watching the crowd move. Hope fights with doubt on his face.

"Will you meet again?" His voice steadies. "If I'm part of this, I want to understand."

"My office is open. Let's set a time next week," I say, handing him my card. The contact is a symbol—one more link in a growing web of witnesses.

He leaves with the card in hand, fading into the late afternoon light. As he goes, a small, serious hope grows inside us both, a small flame against the darkness just out of sight.

Healing Beyond Medicine

Dr. Alex Reid

At St. Vincent's hospital, the air feels different from the busy city outside. Stretchers move smoothly on the shiny floors. A clock ticks above the intake desk, counting the minutes until the next dose of medicine. Light shines through the greenish glass, and the smell of disinfectant is mixed with the smell of lunch and old coffee.

In the children's ward, rules are strict. Everyone watches to make sure no one breaks them. Leaving the rules is seen as a serious mistake. Notices on the walls and the hospital leaders remind us that every treatment must be approved and carefully watched. "If it's not in the rules, it's not allowed here," said Dr. Singh last week. Doctors who don't follow the rules can be punished, moved, or worse. The hospital's managers quietly warn about lawsuits and good reputation. We are all supposed to be scientists, not miracle workers.

Sam Carter's room is quiet and sad. The curtains are open to bright afternoon light, but it feels wasted on him. He looks very sick, pale and fragile, wrapped in sheets and connected to tubes. His mother sits quietly, biting her nails and rocking, hoping for a sign of hope. She looks at me, wanting a miracle I can't promise.

I hold his file—it shows the right diagnosis and treatments. Sam has bad pneumonia that won't get better. Even strong medicines don't help him. His heartbeat is steady but barely.

"Dr. Reid?" His mother's voice shakes. "Is there anything else that can be done?"

The rules say no. If I say yes, I could get in trouble.

"Nurse Patel, could you give us a moment alone?" I ask softly. She nods and leaves quietly.

The blinds close gently. The room feels heavier. Sam's breathing becomes rough. I hold his hand; his skin feels warmer than it looks. Am I crossing a line? The room feels small and close.

Then, a strange feeling begins inside me. Weeks ago, I first noticed this—something deep and unclear. It's not something medicine can explain or prove. But Sam's pulse is quick under my touch; there is no time for tests or rules now.

A dark energy flows from my palm into him, cool like spring water. Sam breathes in slowly, and I feel a tightness in my throat. Am I doing this for him or for myself? Is it caring or breaking the rules?

Color comes back to his cheeks. His eyes open, weak but alert. Relief floods me, stronger than fear or guilt.

The door opens. Nurse Patel and Dr. Harris enter, shocked to see Sam sitting up, his legs swinging, blinking in the soft light. Sam's mother laughs and cries at the same time.

"His oxygen level—" Nurse Patel checks the monitor, voice shaking. "It's at ninety-eight percent."

Dr. Harris looks at Sam closely. "This... this can't be real. He was—"

I force myself to stay calm. "Sometimes pneumonia gets better quickly with the right care," I say, though I don't fully believe it.

Dr. Harris calls for Dr. Singh and the rest of the team. The nurses watch as Sam, cautious and amazed, sits up. His mother holds his hair, crying.

Walking down the hall, I feel cold. Their voices follow me: he fixed the impossible, but he broke the rules. The shadow around me grows, a secret that cannot stay hidden.

Dr. Marcus Flynn

The coffee at St. Vincent's tastes bitter and sharp. I stand beside it, listening to the hospital's quiet hum. Sam Carter's recovery is the main topic everywhere—a miracle, people say. In the pediatric wing, the story moves fast.

Anita Desai counts sugar, her hands shaking. Michael Lawford holds his cup tightly, eyes avoiding me. Their loyalty feels tense and fragile.

"Did you see the charts? Sam was on a ventilator and almost died three times," I say, my words heavy.

Anita looks down. "Nurse Patel said he was sitting up by himself. No one knows how."

Michael breathes out quietly. "They're saying it was Alex. Something strange."

I remember the warnings about breaking the rules after past problems. Sam's sudden healing is hope and fear. What will medicine become if this is normal now? The anxiety grows.

"Let's go," I say, leading them to the staff meeting. The hallway smells strongly of disinfectant. The building feels full of whispers and rumors. As chief resident, I carry many years of rules with me. What happens if one person changes everything?

The staff room is crowded and tense. At the front, Alex stands calm, half in sunlight.

The room quiets and I speak sharply:

"Dr. Reid, you treated Sam Carter. His recovery surprised us all. Can you explain?"

Alex looks calm, with a small smile. "I focused on keeping his oxygen levels stable and supporting his lung function."

I hear a lie in his words. The hospital forbids unapproved treatments, no matter the risk. My anger rises.

"You say 'above all,' but does that mean above the rules?" I ask. "This kind of recovery is unheard of. Did you write down everything? Or is this another secret method?"

Alex's eyes are steady. "I acted for the patient's well-being. That's our duty."

His calm drives me mad. The other doctors shift uncomfortably. Anita tightens her grip on her pen and moves away. Michael sweats nervously. No one speaks. Fear and suspicion fill the room. No one wants to be close now that the hospital's balance feels broken.

"Care for patients or glory?" I ask coldly. "This hospital is built on safety and honesty, not whatever you're hiding."

Doctors start to whisper. Some glance at Alex but quickly look away. Anita pulls back. Only Alex stands still, calm as ever, as if his presence could heal this tension.

"Is this about Sam or about protecting yourself?" I ask. "If you were wrong, would you be so calm?"

"I'm not here to argue," Alex says quietly. "My job is to help patients, even if that means going beyond current guidelines."

The room grows heavy. Fear mixes with duty. If medicine can be so easily broken, what holds it together? Doubts and jealousy rise. I built this tradition. Alex seems to change it all. Rules are the last defense against chaos and wishful thinking that harm medicine.

"You better hope your miracles work, Dr. Reid," I say through clenched teeth. "Because here, mistakes risk every life."

The meeting ends. The supervisors avoid looking at me. Nurses outside look down, whispers full of awe and doubt.

I leave quickly, heart heavy. Rumors follow me: miracle worker, madman, danger. Small groups whisper in quiet corners, mixing fear and wonder.

At the end of the shift, Alex stands alone in the hallway. A young resident looks at him with fear and admiration, then leaves quietly. The hospital's world has changed. My control feels like dust in the cold air.

Emma Thompson

Only two ceiling lights work in the break room. The air is cold and smells faintly sour. The fridge is broken, cups are stacked, and the room feels empty. Alex sits at a table, hunched over, lost in thought. He doesn't notice me at first. My shoes make a small noise as I sit opposite him and curl my knees. The room feels separate from everything else, like a place where reality blurs.

Alex keeps his head down. The quiet hum and distant cleaning sounds fill the space. The clock ticks steadily, matching my nervous energy. I look at the dark circles under Alex's eyes—he looks tired and worried. The space between us feels stretched by too many things left unsaid.

I try to speak, starting with simple words—it's late, you should rest, want coffee? But they don't connect us.

"Alex, what you did for Sam Carter..." I speak carefully, my voice soft. "You stayed with him all night. People talk about miracles, but they don't really know you. I see your hands—they..." My voice trails off. My chest feels tight, wanting honesty but afraid.

His hands grip his mug tightly. He speaks quietly but firmly. "What I did wasn't by the rules." He looks at the table, focusing. "All that mattered was helping Sam breathe. Sometimes, to save someone, you have to cross lines you never wanted to."

"But Alex... what exactly did you do? What's happening to you?" I whisper. "This isn't like what we've learned. You're—" There's no word for the strange power I saw in his hands, the breath he gave back to Sam. Not magic, not science. Something forbidden, frightening, and beautiful.

Alex doesn't meet my eyes. He shakes his head. "You don't want to know. You shouldn't. My only goal is to stop others from suffering if I can. If that makes me reckless, I'll take that. But I can't explain." All the years I've known him feel close and far at the same time.

"Will you tell me if you're in trouble?" I ask, unsure what I hope to hear. A heaviness grows inside me, a quiet fear that won't fade.

He stays silent. His shoulders drop more, his face in shadow.

Time passes. The lights buzz, the clock ticks. I can't stand the space between us. I reach out and cover his cold, shaking hand. "No matter what happens, I'm here with you. I have to be." My voice shakes, and I don't know if it's truth or hope. I'm not sure I'm brave.

He looks up slightly. His gentle, haunted eyes hurt me.

Our hands tight together, the pipes above us groan, as if telling of hidden things. This hospital lives by strict rules. They say unapproved treatments are dangerous and breaking rules is a threat, but no rule can measure the pain of a sick child or the secret weight a doctor carries. Miracles live here, hidden among fevers and antiseptic, in the gaps of hospital policy and whispered behind closed doors. Shadows hide between facts; rules cannot touch miracles or their price.

My thoughts spiral, hard to control. All the years of studying and working hard now mix with suspicion and fear about what Alex is doing. Caring deeply is a gift and a curse: how can someone risk everything—career, soul, sanity—for others? Am I here to watch, to protect him, or to pull him back when the darkness grows too strong? The fear is not just for him but for myself, for what I might lose if I follow him into the unknown.

Still, how can I not hope? Hope that what we share, hidden in the shadows, can survive the doubt and fear that fill the hospital. But maybe hope is dangerous, and believing in him pulls me away from who I thought I was. This hospital isn't made for miracles or secrets that weigh on the heart. I imagine a future where I am either his shield or his downfall, uncertain which the dark will choose.

My hand stays in his until the nurse's voice breaks the silence with news of the next shift. The moment ends. Alex stands, lets go of my hand, eyes unreadable. He walks into the hallway, his shoulders firm, a figure shaped by dusk and quiet strength.

Left alone, I watch him go. My jaw tightens with resolve, but my worry, deep and patient, stays. It's just me and the humming lights now, and the knowledge that every miracle comes at a price.

Friendship and Rivalry

The morning light struggles through the frosted windows of the conference room. Inside, the bright fluorescent lights feel too sharp. The smell of burnt hospital coffee mixes with the clean scent of the rooms. The conference room shows its true side: sweating under starched white coats, soft whispers blending with the hum of the air vent, and eyes catching reflections in the glass wall.

I sit at the end of the long table, my heart beating fast under my shirt. Marcus Flynn suddenly speaks, his voice sharp and cold. He stands tall and thin, frowning like a surgeon ready to criticize. His words hit hard.

"Dr. Reid's so-called plan," Marcus says, "feels less like real medicine and more like a risky guess. Trying a new mix of treatments on a serious patient—without everyone agreeing?" His voice sounds cold and harsh, like old hospital halls filled with fear and iodine. Chairs move slightly, nervous energy spreading through the doctors and nurses listening.

Marcus turns to the group, his voice getting louder. "Should we risk a life on unproven research—and on just one doctor's choice?"

For a moment, every small noise feels important. Even the old clock seems to slow as I prepare to answer. My pulse pounds in my head, and my hands shake under the table.

"My choice is based on evidence," I say, carefully and clearly. "The patient's tests are improving. Recent studies show—"

Marcus cuts me off, his tone dismissive. "Ah yes, today's research. Theory over years of careful practice?" He looks around, as if asking others to agree. His followers nod, confident and cautious, hoping to sway the group.

Some senior staff exchange looks. Some show sympathy, others doubt—deepening the tension Marcus started. The room fills with silence and nervousness. It feels like loyalties shift quickly here. Some eyes watch me, others look at Marcus, weighing who seems safer.

This rivalry isn't new, only stronger now—Marcus sticks to old rules like a weapon, and I keep pushing for change. It's an old medical battle, but now it feels stretched between the usual and the impossible. Some say the hospital itself takes sides when strange things happen, like flickering lights or elevator stalls. Tension hangs in the air, as if the building remembers old fights and lost patients. Even the paintings on the wall seem to lean toward the loudest voice.

Next, we go to rounds. The hall seems to stretch and shift like a dream. My shoes make uneven sounds as the residents follow me. Marcus walks next to me, quietly telling the nurses different orders, criticizing me softly but clearly. "Maybe Dr. Reid's patient should get less new treatment and more of the usual," he suggests. Nurses look unsure, caught between our orders. Decisions split, and the space between us feels thick. One resident pauses near Marcus, then quietly moves back to me, caught in the silent dance of power.

My charts feel heavy, patient cases shifting like unsure thoughts. The hallway lights twist reality, and every word spreads doubt—a quiet chorus waiting to see who will lead here.

This isn't just about one new treatment. It's the old fight between saving and letting go—between hope and caution. Every glance, every comment changes the team's balance. Friendships grow and fade before the clock finishes another round.

Hours later, the doctors' lounge feels empty and sad. Half-finished coffee mugs and old medical diagrams hang on the walls. My hands rest on the table, twitching from being tired. Marcus appears, his eyes cold.

"Hard day, Alex?" His smile feels sharp. "You look tired. Should you be leading the shifts?" He looks at my hands. "Better steady those if you want to make history."

A cold silence hangs. Marcus leaves, his footsteps echoing as the door closes behind him.

I stare at the table, jaw tight, tired but determined. Let Marcus talk. Let them all talk. My body—sweating, shaking, holding something strange inside—is not done fighting. There is still hope in healing, and as long as this fight goes on inside the hospital and me, I will keep going.

Sunlight shines on the tile floor of the consultation room, broken by footsteps and Dr. Raj Patel's shadow by the window. Work has left me empty and tired, but I still follow the routine—patient chart in hand, filled with tough problems. The air smells like printer ink, hand sanitizer, and a hint of my own worry.

Raj's eyes light up when he sees me, noticing I didn't knock. There's something easy about him—he doesn't get defensive when I start talking. Lately, I watch my words carefully, not saying too much. "Can you look at this with me? Something isn't right. The heart monitor shows odd patterns—too much calcium in the blood, but the kidneys seem fine." My voice feels rough. He doesn't roll his eyes or check the clock, just leans in and says:

"Is this the new patient from Riversdale? What meds are they on?"

"Most diuretics were stopped. But I don't like the shadow on the latest scan."

He looks at the images with me. We stand close, sharing the light from the old monitor, and he offers strange ideas—a special kidney test, maybe a new immune treatment not yet approved. I barely notice my shoulders relaxing, feeling a small warmth. "What about allergies to contrast dye? We could try a different MRI scan that is safer."

Raj's questions are gentle, curious, not critical. I'm still nervous—old hurts sting; others have not just doubted me but seemed to enjoy it. Last time someone asked "Why not this?" it was to trap me, not help. Once, asking for an unusual blood test earned me laughter in the breakroom: "There goes Alex, chasing shadows." Every risky move was another strike against me. But not today. Raj's ideas come and go like a tide, not a storm.

We talk late, and I think about trusting him, letting his ideas shape mine.

*

In Operating Room 3, the bright white lights feel unforgiving. The clean sheets, antiseptic smell, and clinking metal fill the room. Sweat pools under my mask. My arms ache. Nurse Naomi stands quietly to my left. She notices my shaking first—moving the tools closer, ready like this is routine.

A clamp slips from my shaking hand. Not dropping—Naomi steadies my hand with hers for a moment. The world feels smaller, the noise replaced by the calm hiss of the breathing machine. No words or looks showing pity. Just trust and movement. This is a quiet bond old as surgery itself—often lost under egos and fear.

Through the haze of pain medicine, the patient's life stays steady beneath my touch. The surgery goes on smoothly. I silently thank Naomi. Her faith is the real healing here, holding me steady, giving hope amid the machines' constant hum.

*

Later, at the staff area, the smell of dry-erase markers fills the air as we stand by the whiteboard—Raj, Naomi, and I, working as a team among busy residents and nurses. My notes, her measurements, his scan ideas—we start building a plan. Raj draws pictures, Naomi writes medicine times in neat shorthand, showing she cares more about patient care than credit.

As minutes pass, I notice looks—eyes full of doubt from memories of past failures. The loneliness creeps up, but the plan grows, moving from one idea to a shared goal. This feels like a win: making something solid that even doubt can't touch. Someone behind me grunts—surprised or quieted.

Coworkers stay, their doubt fading because Naomi knows what I need, and Raj's confidence holds the room together. Their distrust fades in the light of our teamwork, so simple and strong it almost feels like magic the hospital rarely lets happen.

These moments are the opposite of being alone. I remember standing over a patient who was failing, trying untested treatments and failing, earning only sideways looks. But there's another memory beneath—teams saving children no one else believed could live, laughs shared over hospital pizza, moments of awe in the operating room.

Loss taught me humility and limits; rare wins taught me to keep going, even when I expect to fail.

Risk tastes strange: sharp and alive. Hope flows through every touch and suggestion.

*

In Room 214, the lights are dim, the world shrinking to the sounds of machines and quiet breathing. The patient's color slowly warms, like a small sun under tired skin. We stand silently—Raj checking tests, Naomi adjusting machines, and I listen for signs of hope—the oxygen numbers rising into normal range.

The hospital still holds rumors and fights, but here we made a small place of truth from doubt. I glance at Raj—his nod steady—and at Naomi, who gives a slight sign of approval. No smiles break out, but energy fills the space, a quiet force built from struggle and will to try again, together.

As the room grows silent, we leave together—not alone—passing doors where conflict still lives. That small, silent look between us promises: today, something is changing at St. Vincent's.

The hospital hallway glows faintly under tired fluorescent lights that turn every shadow into a bruise and wash color away. The walls change between yellow and sick white. The floors echo with past footsteps, emergency calls, and whispers of loss and hope. Past midnight, time feels flat here—hours blending together. It should be quiet, but the air moves behind me, full of static that makes hairs rise on tired skin.

A sharp pain bursts through my ribs like fire. Patient charts scatter to the floor. My knees give way; my worn white coat feels heavy, pulling me down. Moonlight through a nearby window slashes across the floor, showing dust floating like tiny snowflakes or atoms ready to split. The pain won't let go. My breath comes hot and broken, almost a groan. The on-call room calls—a door slightly open, warm light spilling on the floor. Every step is a negotiation with a body that feels foreign, hands clutching my side, trying to hold myself together.

The cot creaks under me—neither soft nor hard, just accepting. The room smells like fake sheets and old coffee, a sleep that never feels real. Each heartbeat rolls through the pain behind my ribs, thunder in a body that should not fail me. A bead of sweat runs down my neck, chased by fear. If others saw this—the twisted face, the shaky breath, hands that don't steady like before—they'd whisper in hallways, losing trust in me bit by bit.

Inside me, doubt flutters like weak moths against ribs. Is this the end? No heroics, just slow failure of muscles and nerves? What will remain if my body gives out but my mind keeps fighting? Maybe this is how old gods felt—forced off their thrones by forces they could not stop. My right hand presses against my side, harder and harder, looking for relief. The pain fades, then comes back like returning tides. Tomorrow my hands must be steady. Tomorrow I have to explain my choices with reason. Tomorrow, no one can know. Not Emma. Not Raj. No one.

In this temporary refuge, minutes mix with past memories: first days with a pager, watching sunrise over the city, coffee bitter with hope; days pushing past limits, believing momentum could erase doubt; the promise to do no harm, a phrase etched deeper with every ache. Tonight, those rules break like frost underfoot. Reputation is fragile as glass—one crack and the breaks show, like spiderwebs under the surface. Fear grows roots, wrapping around the fact that one day I might have to be kind or cruel to myself.

What if tomorrow my hands shake so much even a new intern sees? What if pain demands attention, taking over? Can a mind trained by years of quick decisions beat a body that fails one cell at a time? Each breath brings different futures—nights where skill wins, diagnosis and instinct working together, coworkers amazed by my calm. But at the edge are colder futures—rooms filled with avoidance, coworkers not looking at me, patients growing nervous in the long pauses before I speak. Reputation and reality: how many lies must this place hold? How long before they notice the healing magic is gone, replaced by tricks?

The door creaks again. Emma's face appears in the window—pale, hair tied back, tired eyes. She enters without asking, understanding without words. Kneeling beside me, she hands me a cold water bottle. Her look is clear, steady. She offers presence, not pity. The water is cold on my tongue—a wake-up call. Her nails are bitten short, her breath smells like lemon. We are both tired creatures of the night, shaped by this strange half-light.

"Bad night?" she whispers softly.

"Not the worst," I answer, lips cracked, voice shaky.

"Need anything?" She sits close, hands folded. The silence between us is care deeper than words.

A long moment passes without talking. In her eyes—gentle doubt and fierce strength, the mixed gifts of those who stay. I remember laughs on cold winter nights, a toast over untouched hospital pizza, guesses about who might break first under pressure. This quiet from her is not judgment. Gratitude bubbles inside me, breaking through the tiredness.

I straighten up, pain sharp but focus clear. "Thank you." Defiance burns inside, strong in my bones. The body may weaken, but the mind and will stay tough and unbroken. Determination grows from the fraying night. What is a doctor but a magician, fighting death with borrowed time and skilled hands?

Emma stands, a hand on my shoulder. We both know she won't say more. The on-call room fades as I walk down hallways lit by harsh, mixed light. Each step is slow and careful. Pain is a shadow whispering behind me. Ahead, dawn waits with its cold hum. Whatever comes, my resolve shines—strong as steel and ready to fight the dark.

Secrets of the Night Forest

A lex Carter

The hospital's light fades behind me as night falls. My fingers grip the worn straps of my backpack tightly, the threads digging into my skin with every movement, making my chest tighten. Nurses' warnings and the quiet stories from the hospital halls replay in my mind—a hundred times they said, "The Night Forest isn't for you, Alex. It's just old tales." But the place behind me feels too small and full of cold, blinking lights. Out here, past the parking lot's noise, the ground softens, and the damp moss smells like old rain and something wild.

Taking a deep breath feels less like bravery and more like a habit. The cool, damp air fills my nose, smelling of fallen leaves and tree sap. With each step, the hospital grows more distant, leaving only memories behind. Tall oaks cast deep shadows overhead, twisting bark hiding old scars. Under these branches, twilight holds no meaning.

The darkness sinks deep into the thick plants and moss, swallowing even quiet words. Roots reach up like hands, brushing against my ankles as if testing me.

Stories about the Night Forest drift like mist. Every nurse knows someone who disappeared; every orderly talks about a relative who changed or never came back. They say something lives under the roots—something older than the hospital, the village, maybe even the earth. Kids dared each other to cross into the woods and touch the oldest tree, but most ran back scared before they reached the shadows. They say a creature watches over the forest, its eyes cold and sharp. Birds call with strange sounds, dusk comes early, and the dark feels thick, like a heavy syrup pressing down on my ribs. The stories warn: don't whistle, don't bleed, don't answer if you hear your name.

Despite the fear, I feel pulled here. A quiet urge inside me, like a question growing restless after many nights staring at strange shapes on my ceiling. This darkness inside me is part of who I am—the reason my hands sometimes glow with black flickers when I'm angry or scared. The hospital called it a sickness; the village called it a curse, but here under these trees, maybe it's a gift.

The path narrows, and my breath becomes short. The bark drinks up the fading sunlight, and the air feels tight, as if the trees lean in to listen. Shadows move by the roots, quick and slippery like fish or slow like spilled ink. My eyes dart around, and my spine tingles. I can't tell if the shadows move on their own or if it's just my nerves. The only sound is something dripping—dew or decay—falling from leaf to leaf in a slow, broken rhythm.

Near a fallen tree covered in fungus, something moves. My heart jumps. Between the roots and rotting wood, a strange figure waits: part real, part impossible, a thick dark shape watching me. Its eyes shine in the dim light, deep and unreadable. It looks at me quietly, weighing secrets in the silent woods. This presence feels heavy, more than just a shadow or body.

I try to speak but can't. The creature moves closer, gliding just out of reach. Its deep voice, neither quite human nor a whisper, fills the air: "Every root remembers the darkness that once walked here." Shadows crawl up my wrists. "And every shadow is shaped by the legacy you carry."

"What do you want from me?" I ask, my voice shaky.

"Want? There is no want. Only unraveling. Light and dark twist inside you, bound by an old promise. You must learn your duties to control your power—or lose yourself in these hungry trees." The words hang heavy and sharp, full of warning. "Ask the right questions," the figure says, stepping back into the dark.

All that remains are the trees, their roots twisting around my boots, the silence growing huge. The forest presses in with the echo of those words. A legacy to understand. A darkness older than fear. My boots heavy with dew, my fingers sore, the forest swallows even the last trace of the Shadow Keeper, as if he were just a trick of the fading light.

Scene 2

Shadow Keeper

Mist swirls over the moss as Alex and I move deeper into the Night Forest, our steps soft on pine needles and damp earth. Old stones covered with lichen glow faintly as night falls. My cloak drinks in the light, shadows clinging like old friends in this haunted forest. Alex stays at the circle's edge, jaw tight, eyes taking in the ancient markers. He feels the warning in the stillness—the mix of rumor and truth held by the roots underfoot.

Here, wisdom and danger are close. Memories fill the cold air: young people struggling with the power in their veins. Many failed, swallowed by the hunger they tried to control. The forest keeps their memories hidden.

A branch creaks. I speak quietly:

"This is where you begin to shape your shadows. Don't see them as enemies, but as part of you. Will you take this legacy?"

Alex nods, swallowing. His hands glow as shadows spread over his fingers like flowing ink. Fear fills the air, sharp like the smell before rain. Hesitation is needed—a warning. The stones remember others who came here, some brave, some scared. They all wanted light to come from dark, but most learned how easily the line fades, how the shadow can turn against the body and mind.

With fingers pressed to a stone, Alex controls the dark with silent words. The shadows shake and twist into shapes he wants—then suddenly grow wild, clawing and striking. The stones remember the pain of loss. I tense, feeling the old ache of failure. The shadows grow angry, and Alex falls to his knees, his skin touching the cold earth. His breath is sharp and uneven, as if he's caught in a storm.

Many before him froze here, afraid of the power that could consume them. My own lessons were learned alone, so deep I felt forgotten—not just by me but by the forest, which erases even bones when darkness wins. Still, I hope to end this cycle: teach control, wisdom, and hope. It is a fragile hope. The children of the night must walk alone.

Alex pushes his hands into the ground, grounding himself. "Don't fight the shadow," I say softly, my words falling like leaves. "Guide it—listen, don't command. The forest knows the difference."

His breath slows. The shadow moves again, gentle this time, responding not to force but to calm. I see a rare light: silver threads start to blend with the dark. Alex's hand shakes, but the shadow doesn't resist. It's been a long time since someone held that small light in the darkness. I feel hope mixed with worry deep inside.

Nearby, a moth beats its wings in the dark, like applause. Alex's power settles, neither conquered nor wild—just present, a friend, not a curse. The forest remembers those few who found peace with their shadows. No one knows what happens to them, but their memory fades quietly, with respect.

Night falls. Cool purple fills the world. The lessons burn in my flesh—each win hard-earned, each failure etched deep. One mistake could mean losing Alex. My hands ache with old warnings: be patient. Shadows move at their own pace. Those who rush fall.

Alex sits on a boulder, pulling out a leather journal. He writes about his stumbles and small victories—naming his fears and wondering what might happen if he loses control. The stones above us hold these memories.

When he finishes, he looks up through the branches where stars shine faintly. He's tired, but pride shines quietly in his weary face, like silver dust in moonlight.

Scene 3

Emma Wallace

Lantern light spreads gold on the brambles, making leaves shine like mirrors. But the deeper I go into the Night Forest, the more the woods close in. Wet earth sticks to my boots, and bushes catch on my jeans like warnings. Every few steps, I stop to pull branches from my coat sleeves. Behind me, the hospital lights flicker far away through the trees. My breath shows in the cold dusk, and my heart beats harder with every crunch.

"Alex!" I call. The wind steals my voice. Shadows jump and slip between roots and tree trunks. They never form clear shapes but never disappear. Sometimes I think I see eyes watching me, glowing in the lantern's light, but when I swing the beam, only bark and soft green moss appear. The Night Forest is a legend—mothers warn kids about it with stories of things that live between dark and light. It should feel strange, but instead, it feels like stepping into a dream, both dangerous and full of promise.

Ahead, branches rustle. I hold the lantern higher. "Alex?" I say, both hopeful and scared. Hope because if he's here, I'm not too late. Fear because the woods are too quiet now, and even my shadow hides in the lantern's light.

He steps out of the dark, hair loose around his face, clothes messy, eyes bright and shocked—and then relieved. If he's surprised to see me, I'm just as surprised. Waiting in the hospital halls felt like carrying a heavy weight that didn't leave room for sense. Seeing him here, alive, lifts that weight.

"Emma—what are you doing?" His voice is low, part worried, part amazed.

"Someone had to make sure you didn't get lost here forever. Besides, you'd be lost without me." I smile shakily, and he laughs, loosening the tight tension between us. For a moment, the thorns don't seem so sharp, and the dark not so cold.

We walk together, our feet sinking into a hollow filled with stones and pale moths. Ahead, a stream sings over smooth rocks, reflecting stars for a moment. A small clearing lies here, surrounded by thornbushes and ferns. You might imagine fairies daring each other to touch the water at midnight. Old stories say this forest swallows memory and hope. But sitting on a mossy stone, knees touching, I feel safe in the quiet magic.

Alex looks at his bruised hands, then at the shadows moving between his fingers. "It's harder than I thought. The Shadow Keeper wants me to make shapes out of the dark, to control it, but part of me wants to run every time." He breathes sharply, his shoulders tight, as if he's waiting for me to be angry.

"The first time, I could only make claws. I almost lost myself in it. Sometimes I want to quit."

Close now, our hands holding the lantern between us, silence humming as shadows creep nearer. "You don't have to do this alone. While I'm here, I won't let you disappear in this place or in yourself." My hand finds his, and it trembles—his or mine, I can't tell. In this moment, with the river singing and our knees touching, trust grows. Maybe being brave isn't standing tall in the light, but reaching out when you're scared and letting someone see. Alex looks at our hands like they're a spell. For the first time, I see doubt fade into hope.

A twig snaps. Something moves through the quiet—the Shadow Keeper. Cloaked in black, his face shaded like dusk, only his dark eyes show any feeling.

"It is time," he says, his voice old and immediate.

From the earth at the glade's edge, a beast forms—fur like shadow, muscles like smoke, eyes burning bright. It splits into two shapes, circling us back to back. Mist swirls around our feet, a chill running through me. I see flashes—losing Alex, trapped alone in hospital walls. My grip on his hand tightens, and the world feels right when he squeezes back.

"We face it together," he says.

Shadows attack, two against two. Illusions spin and double, circling. One whispers old truths—my failures, my smallest wrongs—and panic flares for a moment, but I hear Alex's steady voice and say his name.

"Alex, now—use your gift. I'm here."

His hand glows with shadow and light, threads reaching out. My heartbeat matches the glow. Calm replaces fear, warmth spreads—a quiet fills the clearing. The illusions break, the beasts fade, turning to sparks that rise and vanish into the stars now shining above.

We fall back on the moss, hands still joined, breathing hard with laughter and leftover fear. The Shadow Keeper watches, his eyes full of approval, then fades away.

Alex's palm is warm in mine as we rest, looking up at fireflies dancing. Old stories never told this—the way trust can soften the darkest night, how hope held in linked hands can keep the forest at bay.

Whispers of a Calamity

Dr. Eun Lee

The lights in the main conference room flicker, stuttering in a way that draws every gaze to the ceiling, as if the bulbs could answer for the currents snaking through the wires overhead. My hands find the wooden edge of the table—a real table, not the laminate they prefer for purposes of "hygiene"—and press down to steady my voice. The air smells of burnt coffee and something sharper, antiseptic, lurking beneath the citrus cleanser the night crew favors. No one sits back; no one slumps in their chair. Even those in the back, whose eyes once roamed to their watches, now blink straight ahead, waiting for the next tremor to pass.

Pages and screens compete for attention: protocols in slick plastic sleeves, smartphones gleaming with the blue glow of new emergency notices. Words taste different now: "Mass casualty," "surge rotations," "rolling blackouts." My teeth scrape the syllables at the back of my mouth. Unread messages lodge like grit beneath the skin.

Coughing breaks the silence—someone from Pathology, or maybe Ortho; it's hard to tell. I read from the sheet laid before me in careful, measured tones. Each line is a spell, sampled and practiced all night, cast against panic. "Intake triage will now prioritize respiratory distress, acute neurological changes, and all burn injuries. Surge teams will deploy in twelve-hour rotations, with crossover huddles at both dawn and dusk. All outpatient activity is suspended effective immediately, except for dialysis and chemotherapy. Attendance at these meetings is mandatory."

No one interrupts—not even Oliver Hammond, who loves to object to everything, even protocols on clean handover. The silence itself feels heavier than the clouds gathering beyond the sterile glass. I read the rest—chain of command, emergency cart prep, code red call-ins. The rules are shifting clay beneath our feet.

A clap of laughter echoes too brightly from the corridor outside, someone trying to break the spell, but the sound dies quickly enough. The city's pulse is wrong. Pulse irregular, like the patients who have begun to arrive with pinpricks of light dancing in their pupils, unable to say their own names, memory short-circuited by something electrical that smells faintly of ozone.

When I finish, the room breaks apart in a shuffle of polyester and cheap perfume. The sharp scents of nerves and synthetic coffee cling to my clothes as I slip past clusters of whispered conversation. The hallways are already different. Staff move briskly, carting supplies that squeak on half-oiled wheels, radios strapped to their belts whispering about traffic accidents due to failing signals and cross-town sirens that don't stop howling anymore. St. Vincent's feels like a ship: watertight for now, but battered so hard the seams groan.

In the supply room, Tara Casey is already at work, her voice clear over the clatter of locked cabinets and the rip of inventory printouts. Tara's authority is softer than mine, but it gets results. Senior nurses chart blood products, antibiotics, and wound dressings, marking numbers in red for each that has dipped below the safety line. Juniors push metal trays overflowing with gauze and saline, building emergency carts the way children build cities of blocks—deliberate, hopeful, and desperate.

The room is tight with bodies, cotton and latex, and the whirr of the ceiling fan that does nothing to temper the closeness. Tara calls names, delegates with the grace of a conductor. Supplies for burns here, trauma kits there. Someone asks for more morphine. No one laughs. Sweat beads on my temple, and with each list Tara checks off, the reality sharpens: this is not a drill. Words repeat in my mind, growing heavier. "Prepare for the unthinkable."

Nerves sizzle in the air, sharp as ammonia. Rafael Mendoza finds a corner by the break room coffee machine, voice pitched for privacy. "I've never seen neuro presentations like this, not even with NMO," he says, his accent curling around each syllable as he glances at Karen Yu. She pretends to check her phone, trying to hide the white calculus of fear beneath her calm.

"It's not just us," Karen whispers, sliding her phone so I catch the headline. Grid failures in six cities. Hospital generators failing two hours at a time. "They say it's EMPs. But that doesn't explain the seizures."

Their words spiral around me. Responsibility pinches my lungs, the air heavy with threat. Was there enough time to prepare for what's coming? Would these plans, so carefully drawn, be enough if the lights go dark and never return?

Alex Reid passes on his rounds, shoes whispering against institutional flooring, tablet casting a sickly blue shadow on his face. Machines drone in the background, heartbeat and breath measured in a language older than panic. His phone buzzes and vibrates—one, two, three times—alerts flashing in red: increased alert status, unexplained surges, another warning about electromagnetic pulses. In another corridor, a code blue blares—and someone silences it before the shrillness can ripple through the ward.

No matter how many times order is declared, chaos builds at the window. My own hands tremble, unseen beneath the surface, as Alex stops at the common room's glass, eyes on the city skyline. Black clouds roll in, stained ink pooling across autumn daylight, and below us the hospital hums with voices—sharp, worried, electric with dread. Emergency is no longer the extraordinary; it is the rhythm of this place. Faces, old and young, flicker past—hoping the protocols we've written, the supplies we've hoarded, and the words I've spoken in early light can hold back the world as it unravels.

Dr. Alex Reid

The pediatric ICU vibrates beneath my shoes, the fluorescent lights humming a discordant counterpoint to the rhythm of ventilators and pulse oximeters. Soap and plastic linger under the sanitized air, trying to drown out a sweetness of grape-flavored antibiotics that coats my tongue as I swallow. Each step across the polished tiles drags me into sharper awareness of the ache in my joints—small fires trapped beneath the skin, fanned by the chill that clings to hospital clogs. Smiles are harder to conjure now. My body is a fragile border, and the border is slipping.

Mrs. Guzmán stands hunched at her daughter Lola's bedside. She clutches a juice box, knuckles as white as her eyes are red. The child, five, splayed beneath a narwhal-patterned blanket, watches the shifting tube on her IV pole like a snake in tall grass. Pulling up the chart on my tablet, words swim, coiling and uncoiling like living things. Reading costs more energy every time.

"Her fever should subside soon. We're shifting to the second-line antibiotics. These are stronger—more likely to help with the infection in her lungs," I manage, my throat feeling like river stones tumbling under each word.

Mrs. Guzmán nods, but the hope in her face is brittle, ready to crack at a misplaced gesture.

My hands tighten around the tablet. A white-hot wire slashes through my left wrist, traveling up to my shoulder, quick as lightning. Sudden, sour sweat clings to my forehead. I reach for the nurses' station—metal is cool beneath my fingers and real. Concrete. The world narrows to the slippery cold surface and the hiss of desperate breathing. Vision pulses at the edge—black shapes dart along the walls, details shifting. Something beneath my skin wants out, as if there is a whole other being deep inside me, pressing its ancient palm against the membrane of reality, restless.

The pain subsides, leaving a faint ghost that lingers like a bruise. No one notices, or they choose not to, as my fingers slowly unclench. White-knuckled, I return my attention to the chart, my voice steadier this time, practicing normalcy because survival here demands performance.

A code blue erupts down the corridor—the shrill page splits the air, slicing through layers of fatigue. Nurses rush past, steps echoing, each footfall part of a script repeated too many times. A small boy collapses in room 407. Measures become instinct: gloves snap tight, stethoscope swings proof around my neck.

Inside the room, chaos multiplies. Monitors screech, IVs rattle on steel hooks. My hands tremble, but protocols override fear. My brain catalogs every motion, but my limbs hesitate, fatigue smearing the lines between action and intention. Breathing synchronizes with counting chest compressions, with the hiss of the ambu-bag, the acrid reassurance of antiseptic burning in the air. The crash cart, bright red and garish in sterile glare, looms like a silent sentinel.

Then—the monitors shriek and glitch, screens blinking. A swelling in the center of my chest pulses, dark and unfamiliar. Shadows pool beneath the bed. No one else seems to see their slow, oil-black spread. A thread of whispered words—spoken or thought, I don't know—slips from my lips, and the noise deadens, as though a curtain has fallen. Machines flicker once, then go silent, their alarms erased by a shade that crawls and clings and then is gone. The team doesn't break stride; relief flushes through faces, focus returns.

Is this what saving a life looks like now? A part of me recoils, cold with the memory of other incidents—lights dimming when panic surged, the charge of the unseen waiting to be called forth. How long before it becomes normal? Or before it betrays me, and them?

Afterward, the corridor feels too bright, walls too close. Dr. Karen Yu catches up, stethoscope bouncing, eyes sharp with questions. She hovers in my periphery, her voice pitched just below the hum of the machines.

"Alex, are you okay? You look... off."

"Just tired. Same as everyone," the words fly, as automatic as any suture or prescription. But she lingers, her gaze needling through fabric and pretending and sweat.

Her voice drops. "No, I mean it. You're shaking. You've been avoiding all of us. Rafael's noticed too." Karen's concern is edged with suspicion, or maybe frustration, or maybe both. "If you need to step back, now's the time. The hospital can't afford mistakes."

"I said I'm fine. There are a dozen kids who need rounds." My pulse races, my throat closing up. "Don't worry about me," is a shield—one I press harder against her look.

She exhales, unsure, and walks off.

Two orderlies hustle past. Dr. Mendoza stands at the corner with Karen, heads bowed. Their voices fade behind checklist chatter. Paranoia edges into my thoughts, a nausea worse than illness: how many more days before someone connects the dots? What will they do when shadows answer me out loud?

The exhaust of too many hours, too many secrets, presses between my ribs. My hands ache, knuckles bright red, bones biting through skin.

Sanctuary: a forgotten MRI prep room, thick with the clean iron scent of disinfectant. Here, darkness is only darkness, and quiet is untainted by need. I sink to the bench, my lab coat ballooning out, sweat beading on my upper lip, then cooling, chilling to sticky salt.

In the dimness, the mantra builds—a thread I wrap around myself. Slow breath. Open the hands. Let the throb in the joints ebb, if only for a moment. My heartbeat slows. The hospital's collective dread pounds in pipes, footsteps, unanswered phones, but here there is only this moment, small and vital.

If this body breaks down, what will happen—will the shadows inside me burst free, hungry? What if, instead, I master it, bend it into something that protects instead of destroys? Imagination spins out: headlines, neon, splintered glass, children safe or lost to some silent storm. The world now cracks at its edges; calamity gnaws, and I stand in the middle, unsure if I'm the dam that saves or the flaw that breaks it all.

Sweat cools to ice. One last deep breath, coat tugged straight, spine upright. I step back out and join the living.

Scene 3

Professor Lila Hayes

Arriving at St. Vincent's feels like trying to slip between worlds. Neon lights—flickering a little too irregularly above the glass doors—slice the last golden slant of evening. My satchel knocks repeatedly against my knee, too heavy with papers that hum and vibrate like disturbed beehives. Every footstep on the tiles echoes hollow, sharp with a metallic tang, as though the hospital itself senses the current seeping from the city outside—a low, anxious buzz that pricks the skin.

There is brittle calm behind the reception desk, counterfeit. The young clerk straightens, her badge glinting. My voice comes out tight, urgent. "I need Dr. Alex Reid paged, please. Tell him Professor Hayes. It's urgent." Her hands don't quite pause in their paperwork, but her eyes flicker wide, betraying that everyone here is waiting for shoe after shoe to fall. Dr. Reid. The name turns heads in a hummingbird's flash.

Hospital air clings: antiseptic, and beneath that, the sour breath of desperation, as if the walls are becoming porous, allowing something darker to seep through. Down the corridor, gurneys pass, wheels squealing; every movement a little too fast, as if everyone has begun to run from shadows gathering quicker than dusk.

Following a nurse to Dr. Brooks's office, my mind churns—pages from my folders blur together, equations and spectral charts overlapping with grainy news feeds. Darkness energy surges trace through continents like veins stained with ink: the same correlation repeating with unnerving precision. No one but Alex has eyes to see it. Or maybe he is the only one bold—or desperate—enough to admit the world no longer fits its old skin.

The door closes behind me. Silence thickens in the hush that follows. Alex sits like a man carved from bone and burnt wood, hollow-eyed and wary. The office is cramped, dust dancing in beams from the window shoved high behind half-lowered blinds. The air tastes faintly of old coffee, liniment, and, under it all, winter rain.

Words jam in my throat. I ease the satchel onto the desk, fumble with buckles that always stick. The dossier finds my hands, the cover stark: "Phenomena—Darkness Energy." My fingers tremble. Something ancient and unseen seems to coil in the corners of the room.

Alex studies me, and the space between us feels brittle as salt flats under a new moon.

"Look at these. You need to see what's moving beneath the surface." My breath fogs the air, though it shouldn't. "Every incident on these maps—arteries traced in the same impossible frequency as what's hitting St. Vincent's. Spikes in electromagnetic pulse, sudden neurological collapses. The world's rules feel—loosened. As if laws you and I spent our whole lives believing in are softening at the edges."

The silence isn't empty; it rings, bruising my skull with all the things unspoken. In these moments, it is possible to imagine the old myths were right, that darkness was not emptiness but a substance. That energy with no name hunched at the edge of every world.

He flips through only some of the printouts, hands pressed flat as if weighing down a gust of wind.

"You're saying it's not just us?" His voice smooths glass over panic.

"Not just us. Not just this city. This—whatever it is—doesn't know borders. It bends them. My team tried to find a pattern, but—" The ghost of a sob catches. "It's not a storm you can move around or prepare for. It happens everywhere at once. Sympathetic resonance—we trigger one another just by watching. You more than anyone."

He looks away, chin taut, knuckles white against the papers. In him, I see a drowning man, somehow still fighting to tread water while the tide changes direction beneath. My chest aches, guilt biting through resolve—dragging him deeper into this, and for what? So the world can have one more reluctant martyr?

"You can't be passive, Alex. Master this, or..." Hope wilts. "If you don't try, the next surge may snap the balance entirely. The smallest ripples are tearing through cities already. Power, medicine, memory—rewritten, corrupted, erased."

The world is not ready for that. I am not ready for that, but the knowledge repeats in my gut: readiness isn't a luxury anymore. We are already changed. The question now isn't how to avoid the calamity, but whether there is courage enough left among us to redefine what it means to survive it.

"You think I could stop something like this?" he rasps.

"Not stop. But you have to try to understand it. Shape it—or, at the very least, not let it shape you alone." My breath shudders in my chest. "The cost of doing nothing, or of mishandling what you carry, is a reckoning larger than any battlefield. You're already in the current. All I can ask is that you don't let it take you. Or the rest of us with you."

Our words linger. The hum of fluorescent lights swells, syncopated with distant thunder.

If I had lived another life—or any other life—the burden of knowledge might have been enough to break me. Some days it still threatens to. The truth feels like a fever: sick, cleansing, scouring. Why Alex? Why me? If human law bends so easily, what is left of right and wrong? There is no comfort in being first with a warning no one wants to trust.

He nods once, his voice wrapped in steel and exhaustion. "I'll do what I can."

When I leave him at the window, clouds swelling purple-black above the city, the light has a different density. There are shapes out there only a few of us can trace, and no way left to turn from them.

Love in the Midst of Shadows

Emma Carter

The fluorescent light buzzes overhead, making the break room feel dull and tired. The smell of old coffee hangs in the air, sharp and stale like the end of a long work shift. Shadows gather in the corners, moving quietly between worn chairs and the tired remains of the day. I watch the door, my heart beating unevenly, until Alex comes in, heavy with worry.

His face is pale, almost see-through at the temples, as if something inside him is freezing him from within. He tries to sit quietly on the sofa, but even the soft cushions seem to hurt under him. His hands shake, pale and veiny, folded tightly in his lap as if hiding a secret. There's a nervous energy in every breath he takes.

All day, through long hours that blend together, I tell myself not to be afraid for him. But here, in this empty room, fear sits beside us. It takes up more space than we do.

His voice is quiet and rough when he starts to speak.

"It's getting worse." Each word feels heavy, like dry leaves scraping together. "Waking up is harder. Moving and thinking feel like sand is in my blood." He looks at the floor, his knuckles turning white as if he might break.

Silence follows. The soft noise of the mini-fridge makes his worries louder in the quiet room. He clenches his jaw, trying to name the thing he's fighting—a strange, changing monster both inside and just beyond sight. "Sometimes, I feel like I'm disappearing. Little by little. Everything slipping away." His eyes meet mine, raw and searching.

I reach out, my hand steady even though I feel scared inside. I touch his fingers, giving us both something solid to hold. His breathing slows, and the shaking eases a bit. I wish I could make belief a real thing, something physical.

"I can feel you slipping away." The idea stings sharper than any knife. How easily he could disappear—into himself, or into what the world expects from him. Into the strange magic that haunts the hospital halls, lingering near the beds like an uninvited ghost.

He waits for me to say something that will fix the pain. But words aren't enough some days. Still, I speak because silence feels worse.

"You're more than this body, Alex. More than what's happening to you. Whatever gift or curse you have, it doesn't define who you are." He looks away, his eyelashes shaking. For a moment, the flickering light above feels like it matches his pulse—light and dark, hope and fear.

His shoulders curl in, fragile like moth wings. Sometimes I see his hurt before he can admit it—how he tenses after a hard case, lingering too long in empty halls, haunted by things only he senses. The times he holds himself up, jaw tight, not letting any sign of pain show. In those moments, he's like a boy walking a tightrope with no safety net.

Quiet now, my hand still on his. Warmth passes between us. Even where he's fading, where his body is failing, he is still deeply human. I want to hold on to that, protect it, wrap it in something softer than hospital sheets.

We sit in silence that feels watched by ghosts—history hanging around us like quiet judgment. I feel the gap between his world and mine, made larger by the magic he carries like a fevered dream. But my presence says loud and clear: You don't have to leave me behind, even as you fade.

His faint smile comes from a place I can't reach. The look we share, tired but gentle, carries things we can't say out loud. In grief and love, our bodies learn the same language.

Inside, fear churns. Am I strong enough to stay with him as he weakens, as rules bend around us and the world's logic breaks under his burden? I want to be brave. I want him to see only certainty on my face, but my courage is fragile. Still, I make a promise for both of us.

"I'm not going anywhere," I whisper, holding the promise like a shield. "No matter what happens next, I'll be by your side." The room feels charged with those words. His eyes fill with tears—surprised and childlike. I wipe one tear away, my smallest act of magic.

"Emma," he whispers, tired but thankful.

"I mean it," I say, feeling my little strength grow until it almost fills the room. "No matter what. When you forget how to fight, I'll remember for you."

He laughs weakly. "You make it sound so easy."

"It never is. But we try anyway."

We sit quietly for a long time. The silence feels alive but delicate. There are dangers we can't name. Rumors don't matter here—only heartbeat and hope and the stubborn fact that tomorrow will come, ready or not.

The intercom crackles sharply, calling my name for work again. For a moment, I push my world aside, squeezing Alex's hand until he squeezes back. His grip tells me he'll come back—maybe broken, maybe scared—but still Alex.

I let go, but only because I know he'll be waiting.

Dr. Marcus Flynn

The conference room smells like cold, bad coffee. The lights buzz overhead, harsh and bright against the worn floor. My shoes drag across it, carrying the weight of too many hours. The room is full. People's coats hang on chairs, and hospital badges flash under tired faces. Doctors and nurses sit around me in a loose semicircle, tense like a storm barely held back.

Alex sits across from me, both brave and tired, a shaky glass of water in his hands. The room falls silent as I step up to speak, the scrape of a chair echoing. Medicine used to be clear—rules, books, certainty. Now, strange things slip in at the edges, things we don't understand. The staff feels it too, in whispers and nervous looks.

"My question is simple," I say, my voice tired but sharp. "Why did you continue the Mickelson treatment when the rules said not to?" I try to sound calm, but inside I'm worried. Something strange has spread behind closed doors since Alex arrived.

Alex answers carefully, talking about special situations and unusual observations. His words annoy me. Behind my closed eyelids, I see his hands glowing faintly gold, memories of the ICU's wild monitors, his quiet predictions coming true. It's more than a small difference—Alex brings waves that could wash away our order. People shift; some check their phones, others frown. Emma sits close by, steady but fragile.

Dr. Latham speaks up, her knuckles white. "We heard the rumors, Alex," she says sharply, "that you do things we can't explain. How can anyone trust that?"

No one laughs or rolls their eyes. Even Dr. Patel stops writing. The room feels like a hot pressure cooker, full of doubt and worry. The hospital used to run on trust—built on long nights, shared mistakes, and eye rolls at rules. But rumors about the supernatural, about what "Alex did last night," break that trust. It spreads like rust, turning comfort into suspicion.

Doctors used to fight infection and time, the hard math of chances and supplies. Now, we meet things that don't follow logic. Is this fear cowardice? It's getting hard to tell.

Alex looks at me, hurt but firm. His words don't touch the real problem. "Protocols must change," he says softly, "when medicine isn't enough." What if what comes next leaves medicine behind? The words taste cold and sharp.

Whispers rise again. Emma leans close to Alex, her hand on his sleeve, showing support softly but clearly. My jaw aches from clenching. Before I can ask more, the meeting ends. People move out, and two orderlies exchange a serious look.

The hallways stretch ahead, full of uncertainty. I hear Emma's quick steps as she talks to Lisa Bishop by the supply cart. The walls are thin here; secrets escape. I walk past as Emma's voice rises, firm. "You think Alex is a risk, Lisa?" I want to listen, but I hold back. Emma stands straight, strong in a way I wish I could name.

The elevator dings, releasing Alex with tired eyes, scrolling his phone anxiously. His shoulders tense, mouth tight—some message cutting deeper than my questioning. Hidden texts, maybe. Nobility and danger packed into quiet silence. Rumors float like pollen, settling on white coats and keys. Before, whispered crises were budget cuts or missing supplies. Now, it's shadows where they don't belong.

This is no longer just about Alex—one doctor pushing scary limits. It's about everything we've built, about stopping miracles from becoming monsters. Every new rule, every blur of science and something unknown chips at our foundation. If the outside world breaks down, the hospital must hold, or we all fall.

Evening slips through the security glass as Alex meets Emma under weak garden lights. Their voices mix with fresh earth and cold wind. Their shapes glow softly in passing headlights, moving together with quiet comfort. From a distance, the way they lean on each other sends a message I can't trust or stop.

They walk into the hospital together, side by side. Determined and strong. Somewhere nearby, new rumors gather, ready to ride the next shift's waves.

Dr. Raj Patel

Their voices always have the same edge—broken, urgent, not just tired. Nurses and orderlies argue as Alex and Emma enter the worn staff lounge. Under buzzing lights, the walls show old paint, coffee stains, and the smell of burnt toast. The air is thick with sweat and static—ghosts of work clinging to every chair and corner. Night never erases the day's worry; it never brings true peace.

Alex stands taller than he feels, cheeks pale, eyes smudged; Emma stays close, her hand near his back, but her steady gaze does more than her touch. Their calm stops the noise briefly—then voices rise again, crashing around them.

"He shouldn't be here, not like this!" an orderly snarls, fingers tight on a chipped mug. "The patients... isn't it dangerous?"

"You saw last week! Things moving on their own—no one's safe," a nurse snaps, her voice sharp, full of fear and tiredness.

Alex lifts a hand slowly, asking for quiet—not as a command but a plea. The room softens to a cautious hush, people gripping arms, eyes scanning, waiting for something strange to happen.

"My illness isn't a secret anymore," he says, rough but steady. "Neither are the things I can do, or what's happening here. No one expected this hospital to have... strange forces in the halls. I never wanted this. It's scary for me, too. I just want to help. If you have questions, ask. If you're scared, say so. But let's talk about it now, together."

His words fight the tension in the room. The nervousness eases, replaced by fidgeting and quiet coughs. Here, honesty feels like a small magic, working against fear.

"Why keep working if you're sick?" someone asks gently, more confused than angry.

"How do we know your powers won't hurt us by mistake?" another whispers.

He answers quietly, his face growing lined with memories—nighttime struggles, days when the world seemed to glow with colors or feelings none of us understand. Emma watches him, and the shake in her jaw fades.

No one talks for a moment. This is where I try to steady them—a staff split between belief and doubt, feeling their world shift. The silence is electric, like the air before a storm.

"Listen," I say, calm but nervous, remembering a different crisis years ago—another hospital, another panic. "When the children's ward had a gas leak last spring, Alex was first in. When the power died during surgery, he kept us calm so we didn't break."

Heads turn. Breaths rise and fall. "Many of you don't remember what it was like before we worked together. I didn't believe in miracles then. But sometimes, miracles choose ordinary people—and all we can do is decide if we stand with them or let fear win."

Even as I speak, I see Emma and Alex lean on each other—the way their small gestures show trust, how Emma's steady voice helps others by helping him. Once, pride would have held me back. Now, I feel relief: lessons learned from hard, lonely fights. Support spreads; Alex and Emma bring a strength that breaks down doubt and slowly brings us together.

Nurse Naomi moves quietly with her worn tray, her kindness smelling like cinnamon and cardamom. Teacups clink on mismatched plates, cookies fill the air with comfort, a reminder of home outside the hospital's walls. Naomi's quiet words almost sound like a prayer. "Breathe, everyone. We're still a team, aren't we?" She meets every eye, and for a moment, wounds seem to heal a little.

Chairs shuffle. Someone takes a cookie, another sips tea and sighs, tiredness fading into calm. Soft apologies pass as stories come out—fears and hopes, the strange new days.

The room grows warm with people trying. Alex and Emma step out into the soft shadow beyond the lounge. They sit on a bench outside, backs against the cool wall. From here, I hear their quiet talk, whispers about getting through another day, about thanks mixed with weariness. Their partnership holds the moment together—not with grand words but simple, stubborn togetherness.

"You held up better than most," Emma says softly.

Alex laughs lightly. "Honestly, I get by because someone believes in me."

"Belief works both ways."

Laughter bubbles behind the lounge door—bright and fragile hope. There's still hard work ahead, long nights waiting, but as Emma and Alex sit close, I let myself hope: trust built under pressure lasts longer and burns hotter than fear.

Darkness Rising

Dr. Raj Patel

The hospital feels heavy with rumors. The thin glass windows in the boardroom shake in the wind, and the streetlights outside cast strange shadows on the faces around the table. My coworkers look tired and worried. Alex's hand trembles near a pile of research papers. Naomi sits next to him, folding and unfolding her arms, as if she's trying to protect us from what's behind the locked stairwell doors. Emma carefully opens boxes holding strange items wrapped with string, mixed with gauze and glass bottles. Across from me, people glance silently at each other, unsure and afraid. The crisis fills the room—the world outside feels broken and dangerous.

No one speaks about the soldiers stationed nearby or the angry crowds gathering at city hall, chanting, "No more magic, no more monsters." The news portrays St. Vincent's hospital as a place of danger and betrayal, blaming magic for the problems. Our emails are filled with panic and requests for supplies that never come. This boardroom is our last link to hope. Maps spread out on the table show quarantined areas and failed supply drops. Our research into magic feels strange and almost useless. We try to rely on what we know—epidemiology (the study of how diseases spread), infection chains, syringes, gloves—but the world has changed. It's magical now, and we must adjust or be lost.

Resources are scarce. Every dose of morphine, a strong painkiller, must be traded. Supplies like IV glucose bags disappear quickly. Rumors say some staff bribe others to get what they need. We have a silent rule: don't lose any more patients if we can help it, even though we have so little. Politics complicates things. Leaders distrust miracle cures, seeing them as both hope and danger. We face hard choices: should we accept new allies if it means risking fear or sabotage? The country struggles with the idea that magic might be the only answer, even if it leads to ruin.

Emma quietly moves around, checking the supplies—a blue glass bottle with symbols, a velvet-wrapped disk that seems to absorb light, and tiny gloves she holds carefully. Naomi arranges medical gauze, the strange symbols on the artifacts curling at the edges. Alex looks down, tense and pale. These strange items feel out of place in a hospital, both promising and threatening. Silence falls before we make a plan. No one knows the full cost of these tools or who will use them first.

"What do we have left?" I ask, my voice dry. "Steel and hope. And hope is running out."

Emma looks at me. "We found these for a reason."

Naomi whispers, "What about him? The last trial—he didn't sleep for two nights. His heart rate was sky-high." She looks at Alex with worry.

A chill goes down my spine. "If it breaks him—no one here will risk their life for an experiment."

Alex stands, meeting my eyes. Shadows move around his fingers on their own. "If we do nothing, more people will die. I know the risks. I'll decide how far I go."

Emma stays calm but strong. "Alex knows his limits. But none of us will do this alone, Dr. Patel. That's how we survive." She looks at Naomi. "None of us believed this was possible this morning. But here we are. We adapt together or we fail."

Naomi looks down but nods. Alex breathes out sharply, as if he's holding back something hard. The air is tense but softer now.

Emma and Naomi start dividing supplies. "Two vials per responder," Emma says. "Keep the amulet close. The artifact sets are split—Emma and I take the eastern sector. Naomi, you take the admin hall with Ajay and Ruth." She hands Alex a wrapped disk. No one says more—just the sound of backpacks being packed and zippers closing.

I hesitate over the chart again. Every plan feels like a risky guess. All the science we know feels weak against what flows in Alex's veins. Leadership feels heavy in my head, like a cold metal band. Doubts knock at my mind's door. What if the darkness takes him? What if saving one life costs another? This is the burden I carry, old and new.

I write orders carefully. "Emma, coordinate with city communication to set up a safe house. Naomi, check medical supplies. Alex, watch your intake closely. We meet again at the eastern stairwell in forty minutes." Doubt colors my words, but we hold firm because we must. No one wants this, but tomorrow demands an answer.

We leave the boardroom quietly, the hallway filled with the sounds of night and distant sirens. Outside, the city is silent, fear hiding in the alleys, hope barely alive. We move fast across the tiled floor. We walk together—Alex and Emma ahead, Naomi beside me holding her kit. Backpacks heavy. Streetlights flicker, moths circling the light. We pass the reception desk, past wilted flowers in vases, through the sliding doors, out into a world where nothing is safe, but everything must be risked.

Tonight, unity feels fragile but alive, held tightly as we step into the shaking dark.

Dr. Alex Reid

The Night Forest is quiet and cold. Moonlight filters through bare branches, making silver and black patterns on the ground. Stones form a circle around a clearing, worn and covered with moss. My bare feet touch the cold earth. The chalk lines of the meditation circle are faded from rain, but my hands trace the shapes out of habit. Shadows hide under my nails, waiting. My breath shows in the cold air: breathe in, count to four, breathe out, hold the darkness back. Try again.

The forest smells like earth and slow decay, like the end of autumn stretching into dark hours. Distant animal sounds are faint. Nothing here is mine except tiredness—and the strange power twisting in my hands. I try to keep it inside me, not let it grow wild and uncontrolled.

Weariness goes deep into my bones. My muscles shake just to hold me up. The darkness wants to escape—a storm flowing along my life-line, hungry for a break in my focus. Every failed breath feels like pain in my chest and spirit. "Steady," I tell myself quietly, a promise almost lost in the dark. The edges of everything flicker, my eyes splitting images of trees and stones. I fight for control, for steady ground, for enough strength to last the night. This struggle is always too hard and never finished.

Memories mix with the present, breaking apart at the worst times. The hospital boardroom. Raj's voice rising. His eyes on my shaking hand holding the artifact pouch. The maps full of red marks, arrows, urgent notes. Did he see when I blanked out, lost all focus? My mind went dark—hot limbs, black edges closing in—and when I came back, the conversation had moved on without me.

Emma's worried glance, Naomi's quiet concern—they come back too. Even Emma's hand on my shoulder offered no comfort that I hadn't put them all at risk, that my weakness could be our downfall. Every time the darkness presses in, the fear is simple: this could be the moment I fail, the time I am less than what they need, and the world falls apart.

Power and flesh are not simple, fixed things. But this thing inside me breaks all rules, demanding everything and offering only a taste of control. It would be easier to blame accident or curse or science that failed to fix me. Instead, guilt grows. My team looks at me—Raj with his serious science, Naomi with her quiet faith, Emma with her hope. Does she still believe when I lose control and darkness slips out too much?

Crushed, wet leaves crunch underfoot as more shadows gather. My arms ache from effort; sickness pain blends with deep dread. Breathing again—if only that were enough.

A branch snaps. My heart jumps, and I start to shout, but it stops as Emma steps into the clearing. Her hair is wild with wind and moonlight, her face set with firm purpose. She kneels by me, as if we've shared this circle before.

"Alex," she says gently, her voice calm and clear, "you need to listen to your body. You keep pushing, but your hands shake." She touches my wrist—where the darkness pools, veins pulsing with something beyond blood. Her touch brings shame and a wish for someone to hold this unsteady self without fear.

"I can't stop," I say, my voice rough between need and fear. "If I don't learn control now, someone will die."

Emma's eyes hold mine, strong and clear. "But if you push too far, you might not live to fight again. Remember the times you trusted feeling, not force? Don't break yourself before the world needs you."

The forest grows quiet around us. Branches cover the sky like a dark cloth. Her presence untangles the night's edges—a soft pulse among old stones and wild life.

She offers silence—a space for me to choose, not judge.

I breathe again; steadier, giving in. Shadows swirl on my fingers, thick and heavy. The stone circle waits, old and half-covered by earth. I let the power flow peacefully—inhale cooler magic and push it downwards, not outwards. The darkness moves gently through earth and moss, wrapping the stones like moonlight from below.

It holds this time. A moment of balance, truer than anything made in sterile rooms. My heart pounds, then my knees buckle, stars flashing in my eyes. Emma catches me, steadying me on soft moss smelling of age and life.

We sit in the quiet blue stillness for a long time. The canopy above trembles—shadows and stars mixed, the air thick with possibility and fear. Emma's hand on mine, and I wish it's enough.

Emma

The conference hall lights flicker, casting yellow tones on tired faces that look like masks. The smell of sanitizer and coffee hangs over a crowd buzzing with nervous energy. My shoes click on worn linoleum as I lead Alex forward—he walks slowly, his body tense, eyes red from too many sleepless nights. Cameras flash like guards watching us, and for a moment, every screen shows his silhouette beside mine. We're late. The administrators near the podium barely look up; their faces are cold and set, like people who have already decided what will happen. I feel the distance rising between me and them, my loyalty firm with every step.

Tension fills the room, thicker than the haze outside the windows. Security guards stand near the doors, white badges shining, eyes moving between us and the crowd. The nation no longer trusts miracles—they coil around the hospital's roots, squeezing until the staff cut corners and patients whisper. Weeks ago, Dr. Flynn and I stood side by side, but today his cold, sharp look dares me to blink first.

Alex stands beside me. Murmurs ripple through the crowd—relief and doubt, hope and fear mixed together. My hand on his elbow is steady, a sign of defiance.

Dr. Flynn speaks first, his voice full of strong feeling but shaped by sleepless worry. "This hospital lost four patients last week—four! And we're told to trust the darkness and powers we don't understand? How much more are we willing to risk? How many more mistakes?"

He gestures broadly, anger and exhaustion clear. Others nod—some serious, some just tired. His bruised eyes, once like mine, look at me now with accusation. The room feels hot and tense, like summer before a storm. I flinch as Flynn looks at me, then Alex, as if searching for old loyalty but finding only betrayal.

Alex stands taller. His voice is low but strong. "We are all scared. But yesterday, in Room 312, you saw Marisol—her heart stopped. I used my power to clear the blockage and start her heart again. When the power went out in the pediatric wing, these shadows kept the incubators warm. Not every result is perfect, but neither is every tool made of steel or code."

As he speaks, the darkness seems less like a threat—as soft as moonlight on water. Shadows curl from his wrists, barely noticed like breath on glass. Some people shrink back, but others lean in, like children hoping to see a magician's trick. I watch Alex's shoulders stay steady, strong, refusing to apologize for being alive and still fighting.

The mood shifts. Quiet doubt turns into something scared but hopeful. Despite my will to stay strong, doubt creeps in. What if one mistake costs too much? How many times can wonder turn to fear before we break? Pretending to be strong is easy until the room creaks and you wonder if you can really hold it up.

A senior nurse, Ms. Gupta, known for being strict, stands. She puts her fingers to her lips and clears her throat. "He saved my son. The burn could have blinded him. The darkness eased the pain and sealed the wound when nothing else could. I trust Dr. Reid." Her voice shakes, but her words shine like a light in fog.

Then a junior doctor, Callum, stammers, "Not a week goes by without someone saying it's hopeless. But Dr. Reid kept my sister alive when she crashed on the way here. We need help—every kind of help we can get."

The hospital staff divides in front of me: some grateful, some afraid. Alliances shift under the dim light—hope and fear stand side by side.

Flynn's mouth tightens. Our friendship was built on shared doubts, on medicine's long path, and the hope that every life could be saved if we learned fast enough. Now his tone is cold, stiff with hurt. For a moment, his eyes ask me to reconsider, but I have made my choice.

People watch me, waiting to see if I will give in or stand tall. I reach for Alex's shoulder and press my hand there. His skin is hot with fever and the tremble of power. I whisper words only for him: Don't break. Not now. Not here. No one knows how much has already been lost, how much depends on a few people standing between disaster and surrender.

Dawn colors the windows pink and shadowy. Cameras click softly like insects. Silence spreads, thick and unsure. My hope is fragile in this hard light, but I will not give it up. Even if the crowd breaks, even if old friendships fall, this moment—I claim it. I won't move. Not for them, not for the fear hidden deep inside.

Battle at the World Disaster Zone

Dr. Alex Reid

At the edge of the disaster zone, the air tastes like ash—sharp and bitter on my tongue, sTicking against my teeth as I breathe in dust and fear, burned trees lean like old men in the wind, dark shapes against a dull orange sky. The city in front of me is no longer a city—just piles of broken glass and twisted metal, remnants of what used to be homes. Empty windows look like eyes left to grieve. Sirens mix with the cries of the injured—too many voices to count, their pain drowned out by a constant rumble from the earth.

Smoke curls around my coat sleeves like a living thing. My boots crunch on rubble as I walk through the ruined hospital parking lot. Survivors, tiny and scattered, lie as if they were tossed by a careless hand. Some crawl toward red rescue lights stuck in deep potholes, while others lie still, pretending to rest. Each face tells a silent story. Dirt covers their skin; hair is tangled with glass, blood, and soot. This scene wasn't created by brushes but by disaster—no place untouched, no family spared.

Before disaster spread like a fever, each city had its own heartbeat—proud, loud, and full of light. Now, only scars remain across continents. Bridges fall into rivers, highways break like bones, and forests lie cut down and rotting. The land is poisoned beyond healing; seas boil with dark water, crops fail, and animals roam the streets looking for food, disappearing under falling buildings. This world is broken—every world is. Volcanoes spew ash, towns are lost in sinkholes, and coasts flood. The disaster connects all souls in a dark blanket. Fear is heavy, sticking to the skin and mind. Days blend together. Sometimes I wonder if the sun even knows how to rise.

Crowds at the disaster's edge watch helplessly, their prayers mixed with falling dust. Police with wild eyes toss water to women crying with grief. Their faces ask: Is this the end? It's no longer just about saving the few hundred in front of me. Now, the whole of humanity is at stake—millions hidden behind walls and hope, waiting for mercy from no one.

I feel a cold power inside me aching to be let out. My body struggles, muscles tightening from the sickness within. Still, I push aside fear, raise my hands—one finger after another—until darkness flows out quietly, like mist. It pours from my sleeves, a black energy glowing violet, gathering above the shaking hospital. Steel beams begin to fall, aiming for a group of medics sheltering nearby. My shadow forms a shield—glowing, smooth like oil but warm like wool. Dust and bricks fall and bounce off harmlessly.

My heart pounds not just from effort but from the weight of so many watching and counting on me. Inside the hospital, scared people

I've helped look to me. Their hope is a heavy burden, almost as sharp as despair; these small moments of trust weigh more than any falling beam.

Then, a road explodes—a broken gas pipe bursts into flames nearby. Red and blue fire spills out, heat burning my face, hair smelling of smoke. Shadows rise from me, swallowing the flames, soaking up the fire like water down a drain. The fire tastes bitter, but the people behind me are safe.

Before I can catch my breath, the ground shakes, cracks open, and mutant vines with sharp silver thorns crawl out. They lash at children, mothers, anyone too slow to run. Panic twists my insides—this is disaster at its worst, the world becoming strange and cruel, nature turning wild with pain. Exhaustion flows through me, but the darkness inside fights the vines, wrapping their thorns in coils of shadow and pushing them back into the cracks. Screams turn into shouts of hope.

From the center of destruction comes a low roar—a deep, unnatural sound shaking the ruins. A black storm churns on the horizon, too dark to be natural night, pulsing with strange life. The world holds its breath. Every survivor and medic looks at me. I'm not ready, but the choice is made: I must step forward, into the storm, into what must be done.

Steel and stone crumble beneath my feet. Ambulances lie overturned, bridges covered in flame-like fungus, and road signs twisted as if by an unseen force. Smoke burns my throat, but I am stronger than fear. My mission is clear. The only way is forward, into the core.

Standing at the storm's center, swallowing my fear and purpose, shadows flicker at my feet—both helpers and burdens. My hands shake, but I steady myself—someone has to face the heart of disaster. This time, for everyone.

Emma Clarke

Blocks of broken concrete cover the road, still warm from fires burning neighborhoods. The air tastes like ash and something worse—magic that smells like burnt ozone, sour on my tongue. My shoes stick as I run, dodging broken wood and strange vines that move on their own. Alex's darkness curls along the horizon with distant thunder, and for a moment, his presence anchors me. The worn leather of my bag presses against my side; every zipper and snap reminds me of what I carry: faith held in bandages, hope in medicine and tools.

Children's cries break the uneasy quiet after another blast. Three children huddle under a bent street sign, faces streaked with dirt, holding each other. The smallest boy's ankle is twisted painfully, visible through broken wood. His older sister presses her hand against a cut on her forehead. Sweat runs under my mask as I kneel calmly. "You're safe. I'm here. Listen to my voice." Years in busy hospital wards and rushing ambulances taught me how to bring calm to chaos. My hands check pulses and wounds like second nature. Their warm skin and beating hearts tell me there's still time.

A toppled delivery van glows with Alex's shield, dark and silver-blue, stopping it from collapsing as he fights the destruction with powers I don't fully understand. Some children glance at it, eyes wide with fear and wonder. They should be scared, but the darkness around Alex seems to protect them. The feeling grows quietly inside me each time I see him risk everything for us.

Dr. Raj's voice cuts through nearby, strong and clear. He is steady, a fixed point in the chaos. "Team Bravo, move! Clear that path! One at a time!" His orange vest stands out against the soot as he guides rescuers through fallen concrete. Radio in hand, he moves urgently but controlled, not letting tiredness show. He nods at me—a silent message from years spent saving lives side by side.

A scream comes from the subway as the ground shakes again. The evil vines glow green and grab at a firefighter, nearly pulling him under. Raj warns, "Front lines, be careful! We don't know what the fog does yet. Emma, how's triage?" His radio crackles a quick update meant for me and Alex, who shields the hospital's ruins. We exchange a look filled with trust: you take that side; I have this one. No matter what, we keep going.

The fog creeps along cracks, sticky and shining, moving from lamp posts to the ruined radio tower. Nurse Naomi laughs, bold despite everything, in the triage zone. Our team made order from chaos, helping survivors onto tarps while volunteers carry the wounded from danger. Naomi meets my eyes, rolling gauze in her hands, giving a quick two-finger salute—our unspoken language: not enough medicine; get more splints; if you're breathing, there's hope. Her support is quiet but deep, the same nurse who helped me in early shifts and patched me up when I was too proud to admit I was tired.

From my low spot beside the children, the world sounds distant, like inside a shell. But when I stand, the wind stings my eyes, and everything sharpens. Naomi, Raj, and I meet beneath the broken awning, dust swirling as the earth shakes again. Naomi picks up a stick, Raj grabs a piece of curb, and we begin to sketch a plan on the cracked concrete: block the storm from the last safe shelter, reroute survivors, use old streetlamp wiring to create a magical barrier. We find each step with almost no words, knowing how to cover for each other's weak spots. This is muscle memory from every emergency call, now stretched to fight something beyond any medical crisis we've seen.

Raj's hand presses my shoulder for a moment. "We've got this if you're here, Clarke." Naomi's knuckles brush mine, a playful spark in her eyes. "One more miracle, Em." We share a look, remembering normal hospital life—bitter coffee in the break room, Naomi's half-finished crossword puzzle, Raj's wild tie collection. Those memories show in our faces, in how we move as one trained team.

Alex bursts through the dust, tiredness clear in every line of his face. For the first time today, there's a stillness. I take his hand—warm, shaking, and familiar. "We're with you," I say, my voice steadier than the ground beneath us. Everyone nods—Raj, Naomi, our small army. The storm behind Alex pulses, black wind threatening to tear the sky, but our circle stands firm as the earth roars beneath us.

Dr. Alex Reid

The wind cuts like sharp knives, filled with rot and decay. Each gust scrapes my cheek, and the roar at the disaster's center drowns all other sounds. Ahead, the disaster core moves, oily and alive, casting twisting shadows over the ruins. The storm rises—black, slick, and unnatural. My boots crush glass on burned concrete. Sirens are gone. Only the screaming wind and disaster's terrible pulse remain.

The darkness inside me rises, flowing through my veins to my hands—ready, eager, almost hungry. Control slips like sand through sweaty fingers. With each surge, doubt pulls at me. Seeing the ruined hospital wing and twisted bridges makes me wonder if I'm enough, broken as I am. The sickness waits, and every new pain feels like betrayal. Even now, facing the end, I wonder: what if the darkness takes me? What if I lose control?

Wind slams into me, thick and burning. Barbed shadows lash out, grabbing at my coat and mind. Lightning flashes—no real lightning, but a memory of it, carved into the air. Shadows crawl into my head, whispering: You're weak. You'll fail. Let go. My knees almost give out. Gritting my teeth, I steady my breath. The darkness swells in the fear-filled hollows inside me. The air smells of burnt metal, ash, and rubber. I taste dust and despair with every breath.

At the edge of disaster, I hear Professor Hayes's voice in the roar—a memory of her teaching: "You must find balance, Alex. Darkness only destroys if you let it. Shadow means nothing without light." The Night Forest—quiet, the silver water flowing over moss, moonlight making patterns on leaves. Those nights when darkness bowed to gentle light, brought out by warmth nearby. Emma's soft laugh, her hand in mine as I stumbled.

All those lessons. Lost patients. Shaking hands under harsh lights, disease pressing against my lungs. The first time I healed with shadow—power mixed with fear—nobody understood my struggle. Not even Raj, not even Emma. Every success felt borrowed, taken from a future meant for stronger doctors. But Emma whispered: "You are more than your shadow, Alex. You don't have to fight alone."

Suddenly, a shadowy tentacle from the storm strikes close, heat burning my face and air twisting. My darkness rises, forming a shield, but it's wild and hard to control. Control slips. Others might break, but I hold on, stubborn. Why give this power to someone so fragile? Why give it if it might betray me?

I steady my pulse—in and out. I imagine the Night Forest's quiet. I listen for the water flowing beneath the storm—a promise in the dark. Deep inside me, past pain and doubt, a gentle pulse stirs—not cold shadow, but something fragile. The light I thought lost, maybe never had. It waits quietly, ready to be found, not forced.

With hands open, I let both exist: darkness, heavy and familiar, swirling in my palms; light, soft and delicate, touching my skin. Shadows twist, but instead of hiding from the light, the light weaves through them like golden thread in black silk. My skin tingles; my heart pounds. The two forces join, neither stronger, spiraling together. From somewhere, Emma's voice comes: "Trust yourself, Alex. All of yourself."

A glowing swirl forms—threads of night and dawn, shadow holding light. It crackles with warm energy in my hands. The storm's core senses this and shrinks away, twisting harder as if it knows the rules have changed.

"What are you waiting for?"

"Nothing. Not anymore."

I raise both hands, feeling my hurt and hope together, and throw all my power—this mix of everything I am—into the disaster's heart. The light roars—not blinding but soft—carrying the forest's quiet and the hospital halls' steady hum. Darkness blends with it, steady and protective. The swirl breaks into the storm's center, and things crack like glass breaking, roots snapping in frozen earth. Shadows pull back. The world breathes cool air as the black storm breaks apart, letting in gold and blue daylight.

I fall to my knees on broken ground. Shadows flicker weakly at my feet. The world steadies. Above, sunlight breaks through the fading gloom, warm on my face—the first taste of hope.

Light and Shadow Together

Dr. Alex Reid

The hospital lies in ruins, its frame exposed, with metal rods sticking out like broken fingers. Broken concrete piles on top of each other, marked by black scars from fire. Beyond the twisted metal, faint cries of survivors inside the collapsed wing mix with the sounds of sirens. The smell of burnt air sticks in my mouth, sharp and bitter. Sunlight hits floating ash, making the sky look hazy and restless. My tired muscles tremble, but there's a strong feeling in my chest—both dark and bright—that pushes me forward.

My hands rise, heavy but focused. Shadows move beneath my skin, cold but no longer threatening; now they are eager and ready to help. Along with them comes a warm, silver energy that runs through my palms and down my fingers as the darkness and light mix. I send this power into the rubble. A small fear from childhood—losing control and feeling pain—flashes for a moment. The sickness, the tiredness, the shaking in my left leg—they don't matter now. The world is broken open, people are calling for help, and I'm the only one who can act.

The shadows sneak into cracks in the concrete where light doesn't reach. The rubble is filled with decaying dirt and purple rot that trembles when my darkness touches it. At the same time, I send out healing light, fresh and sharp like pine after rain, cutting through the heavy, burnt smell. Dust settles as stone and metal join back together with a low hum that vibrates through me. The wall moans, then stands tall again as broken parts mend—both stone and flesh. Inside, a child's cry turns into sudden laughter.

Grass at the edge of the damage shakes, then straightens, its green color becoming bright and strong. Poppies coated with ash bloom stubbornly in cracks, their red petals bold. Thin dogs with ribs showing walk into the warm light and lie down, letting out contented sighs. The soot rises from the cracked sidewalk. Even the earth seems to breathe again under my touch. Part of me wants to collapse and rest, but the hope I see in the volunteers keeps me going—stronger than any pain.

Emma stands near the triage tent, her hair tied back, sweat and dirt on her face. She calls out orders sharply, her hands steady. "Bandages here! Naomi, start chest compressions—Sam, give more water!" Dr. Raj Patel moves calmly through the injured, always searching for a way to help. He leads a group that moves carefully, like one body, through the wounded. Everyone involved—helped by this mix of magic and medicine—stands taller, and laughter mixes with cries.

"We need another stretcher here—move! Alex, are you..." Emma's voice breaks when she looks at me.

"No stopping now." My voice is weak, but the power grows. Her trust gives me strength; it is like a warm anchor among the ruins.

"Keep steady. Focus!" Raj pushes us to work together, as if we are the heart of the city trying to beat again.

Supplies move hand to hand. Volunteers' arms are cut and bruised but don't stop. There is a rhythm now, a pulse that connects us all—my magic flows through their work, their hope feeding me in return. Near the edge, the old stream that was dry days ago flows again, clear and fresh over stones. A girl drinks from a cup, cold water running down her neck, laughter bright and infectious.

The air no longer smells of fire. Instead, it carries hints of wild mint and pine, plants lifting their leaves to the sky. Emma's team cheers as injured people—faces dirty and eyes wide with surprise—sit up, reaching for each other. Their thanks fill the city's broken frame. Men, women, and children move closer, some crying openly, hands pressed over healing wounds or held in quiet prayer.

Their eyes show awe—not the kind that worships but the kind that connects. In this moment, my powers—the shadow I once feared, the light I don't fully understand—become something not scary but necessary. Something shared. The line between miracle and hard work is gone.

Not long ago, my illness made me feel broken, a risk in life-or-death moments. Some at St. Vincent's watched me with anger, jealousy, or doubt. Now, survivors—hospital workers, strangers, friends, and even rivals—move with me as if linked by an invisible thread. It feels like the whole city breathes with one lung, hearts beating together.

Responsibility feels heavy. Fear is still in my mind; what if the darkness flares out of control? What if my sickness takes over again when I'm weak? But quiet, molten resolve rises—like sunlight breaking through clouds. The worst is over, nerves raw. My shaking hands hold loss and hope at the same time. The tiredness is a badge I won't give up. Today, I'm more than my illness—I am medicine, shadow, and light.

Clouds part above, sunlight spilling over the fixed block like honey. Birds call from window ledges, awkward and sharp, and a cool breeze moves through what's left of my hair. In this quiet, the city stands—wounded, glowing, and very much alive.

Emma Clarke

Evening glows softly over the damaged garden near St. Vincent's; cherry petals drift at our feet—some in tangled grass, others floating over mud where flowers are just starting to lift their tired heads. The world hasn't been whole for long. I hold Alex's hand—not lifting it, just holding it—and the warmth steadies me in this growing calm. Our shoes scrape cracked stones and overturned benches. The hospital's broken windows gleam in the sunset; past the garden fence, the Night Forest holds its secrets, mist curling at its roots like breath.

We stop beneath a cherry tree. Only hours ago, Alex fixed what was broken, healing the world's wounds with magic as real as any medicine I know. The breeze pulls loose hair from my ponytail as he looks up—eyes stormy but now soft, worn thin but true. His voice is quiet here, with no need to be strong for others.

"Sometimes," he says, thumb brushing my ring finger, "it feels like there's no end to what needs fixing. I want to do more, always. What if it's never enough? What if the sickness comes back, worse this time? What if—" He stops, looking at the bruised flower above, "what if I can't hold this balance? Healing with one hand, darkness in the other. What if I hurt someone?"

There's a small shake in his voice, so light most would miss it, but I know him well—the cost of every miracle, every sleepless night, every time he pressed a hand to his chest like it might fall apart.

"Alex, listen. You're always the one running toward the broken places. You shine in Emergency—it's not just your power; you'd be here even without it. That's who you are." I speak steadier than I feel. "I haven't told you, really, but I want to be that too. A doctor. I want to help like you do. I'm scared, but I want you to let us—let me—in when you're scared too. Don't keep shutting me out to protect me. We're past that."

His head drops. Cherry petals fall in his hair, but he doesn't brush them away. The way he stands—scarred hands, open palms, his jacket slipping off one shoulder—makes it easy to see his cracks and how strong it is that he's here.

The wind carries the sweet smell of crushed camellias and lavender—signs that softness still exists, even in a world that seemed ruined hours ago. My wish grows inside me, bright as starlight, reaching up. If he lets himself be loved, if he dares to lean on me, maybe we can both stand taller. Maybe we can heal each other where it hurts.

Alex lifts his head and breathes slowly. "No more hiding. Not the illness, the shadows in my veins, or the part of me that fears what people think if they know how broken I am. If you stay, if you mean it, you'll see it all." He smiles softly, eyes wet. "I don't want to pretend for you. I trust you, Emma. Completely."

His hand slides into mine—not trying to pull me, just fitting. His pulse is quiet against my wrist. "Whatever happens," I say, my voice stronger than I feel, "I'm not leaving. Even if you try to send me away. You showed the world how to heal even while hurting. Let me show you how to rest in someone else's care."

That love hits me hard—bright and messy and a bit scared. His tears fall; laughter escapes me, rough and real like dirt under my nails.

We hold each other right there in the muddy row of flowers. He lets his jacket fall. My nose touches his neck—smelling of sweat, ozone, fresh grass, and the rain's last scent. Sunlight paints our faces through the trees as he holds mine. His scars show now, sleeves rolled back and shirt undone at the wrist. Nothing hidden, not even shame. Our eyes meet, and the old distance between us—colleagues, friends—is gone, burned away in the deep quiet of dusk.

Silence falls gently. My fears rise: what if the disease grows worse, what if the darkness asks too much from Alex? But hope grows stronger. The thought of learning medicine together. Being the reason he laughs on tough nights. Fighting not just for patients but for us, even when running away would be easier.

When we finally sit—elbow to elbow, fingers tangled—the garden feels peaceful like a blanket. Fireflies spark near the flowers, rising over the wet grass. The Night Forest stands guard, shadows and mist creeping into the edges of this new world. But here, right now, there is only the promise of healing hearts and quiet, steady love.

Professor Lila Hayes

Evening spreads colors like stained glass over the lake at the special time when the Night Forest breathes out shadow and the day's last light catches fire on the water. My shoes crunch softly on reeds and moss by the water's edge. The silence is so complete that even the air barely moves. Across the smooth lake, dusk folds gently, wrapping the world in velvet. There—where reflection meets real—Alexander Reid kneels, his body outlined against the dark orange and purple sky. His shoulders are square, his back straight but flexible like a willow branch, able to bend or break with the wind or his will.

His hands rest on his thighs, palms up. Shadows flow over his feet like small fish. Each breath brings the cool, wild smell of wet earth and pine sap—steady and calm. The Night Forest surrounds us, its trees forming endless dark shapes. Alex looks smaller than when he healed disaster, but not less strong. The lake shivers once; clouds move, showing the first star.

A doctor born with sickness—whose body never fully gave up, even when others turned away from pain. But what is pain but a message? Alex has learned to understand it and respond gently. Tonight, his jaw is relaxed, peaceful. My heart tightens a little as he closes his eyes and bows his head.

Brown and gold streaks move across the lake, showing the far sunset fire. Then, in the water's mirror, his image changes. The line that once split light and shadow on his face is gone; no more war between them. Instead, one glowing shape forms, golden light wrapping into soft shadow, both parts joined naturally like breathing. It's transformation—the kind that accepts both softness and strength, healing and harm. For a long time, he thought one side would cancel the other. Now, they are in harmony.

It's a strong mix of wonder and pride. How many times did his hands shake, afraid he'd become the disaster instead of its cure? How many nights did he press his fists against his ribs, scared of the darkness in his veins? I remember the boy on the ward, feverish and burdened beyond his years. He has pushed away pain before but never accepted it.

A twig snaps gently nearby, breaking the spell as I step beside him. The moss is cool under my feet, the lake wrapping us in a circle of amber and purple light. Alex's eyes open slowly, like waking from a deep dream. For a moment, both our reflections move in the water—teacher and student, shadow and light.

"You've found it," I say softly, not to break the calm but to honor it. "You have accepted all parts—the pain, the power, the hope." My voice catches with feeling, but I don't hide it. "That is true healing, Alex. Medicine can fix bones, but you've learned to heal all the broken, wild parts inside yourself." Silence falls again, broken only by distant nightbird calls and the lake's smooth surface.

He stands up, knees creaking. The scars on his hands catch the warm light, neither hidden nor shown off, just there. Alex meets my eyes, and in them, I see thanks and strength, a storm calmed at last.

It is hard not to remember every test—the first shaky tries to use his power, the fear, the chance of losing himself. The shadow scared him more than any sickness. Yet here he stands, and in his stance, a new strength flows.

What will this balance bring? Thoughts spin, opening possibilities as night deepens. Maybe as Alex moves forward, his touch will bring peace—not just to bodies but to hearts weighed down by pain, to coworkers who only trust what they see and measure. If new dangers come—natural disasters or dark forces—maybe he will meet them whole, not broken in two, fully human.

There is hope, sharp like a pine needle, that people around him will see themselves in his light and shadow and let their strengths and sorrows come together instead of breaking apart. The boy who once refused help now builds a life where darkness lives beside kindness, neither banished nor in charge. My role—once teacher, now something quieter—shifts too. I must trust his strength and let go, as every parent or teacher must eventually.

The wind stirs, carrying smells of peat and wildflowers, and the Night Forest feels less scary. Stars appear, first a few, then many. Alex looks toward the woods, face lit by moonlight, shadows and gold mixed on his skin.

"That feeling," he says quietly, "it's not fear anymore. Not defeat. Just... belonging."

"We carry all of ourselves, Alex." My hand rests on his shoulder, warmth shared in the growing dark. "That's how we move forward."

He nods. I let go, and he walks onto the lakeshore path—shoulders straight, a silver outline, stepping into the unknown, balanced between shadow and light.

Epilogue

The Night Forest was quiet.

The wind moved gently through the trees, carrying the scent of earth, rain, and something ancient—something waiting. Alex stood at the edge of the clearing, feeling the last threads of darkness coil beneath his skin in soft, familiar spirals.

He was no longer afraid.

The hospital's chaos, the accusations, the cold stares... they felt like echoes now. What once felt like a curse had become a burden he understood, a power he could shape instead of hide.

Behind him, footsteps approached—soft, steady, sure.

Emma.

She stopped beside him, her warmth dissolving the last of his fear. "You're not alone," she whispered.

For the first time, he believed it.

The shadows shifted across the trees, bending gently toward him like a bow.

Not consuming.
Not demanding.
Awaiting.
Alex took a breath that didn't hurt, that wasn't heavy with secrecy
or guilt.
A breath that belonged entirely to him.
"Then," he said quietly, "let's go home."
And together, they stepped forward—
into the light,
into the future,
into the truth of who he had become.

Final Thoughts

Every story begins with a heartbeat—and this one began with a doctor who wanted nothing more than to save lives. But healing often demands more than knowledge, courage, or strength. It demands sacrifice. It demands truth. And sometimes... it demands facing the shadows we fear most.

Thank you for stepping into this world of medicine and magic, rivalry and love, darkness and hope. May you carry with you one simple reminder:

Even in the deepest night, your light still matters.

Review Request

Thank You for Reading!

Your support means the world. If you enjoyed this book, would you leave a quick review? Even one sentence helps other readers discover the story.

**★★★ CLICK HERE TO LEAVE YOUR REVIEW ★★★